Praise for J.D. Austin's
What You Find in the Woods

"J. D. Austin's book of short stories, *What You Find in the Woods*, stands as another proof of his amazing talent. His stories come to the reader as gritty and authentic as real life. Through his broken characters, he imparts age-old wisdom set within the homey and raw landscape of the northern Midwest. These stories take us into the minds of young men and women who live within the purgatory of becoming broken."

— Sue Harrison,
international bestselling author of *The Midwife's Touch*

"These are stories Jack London might have written, if Jack London had been an opiate-addled ex-hockey player. *What You Find in the Woods* is about how we grieve, and how death surrounds us wherever we are. Throw in a car chase and a couple of beer jags and you have the literary equivalent of gelignite. Austin reminds us of the importance of homemade grilled cheese in nursing homes, of the dangers of the 'day-murdering nap,' and the fact that nobody's free until the day after they die. These are powerful stories that Hemingway himself would have been proud to have written: they have the same coiled energy as 'The Killers' and 'A Clean, Well-Lighted Place.' *What You Find in the Woods* does for the Upper Peninsula what *Knockemstiff* did for Ohio: J. D. Austin is a bright, scathing talent."

— Sebastian D. G. Knowles, Professor Emeritus of English,
The Ohio State University

"J. D. Austin's new short-story collection, *What You Find in the Woods*, offers a diverse set of tales, some short, some really novellas, that reflect the grittier side of life in Upper Michigan, especially for young millennial men seeking to survive while coping with issues like loneliness, heartbreak, and alcoholism.

Austin creates realistic dialogue and even more realistic characters as he delves into the intricacies of the human experience, trying to make sense out of a world where sometimes we are our own worst enemies."

— Tyler R. Tichelaar, PhD,
award-winning author of *The Mysteries of Marquette*

"…with his two opening stories plus the powerful titular story set midway—even though poor Jake was a goalie in hockey—Austin scores a 'hat trick' for the book. Well-made and exciting stories. And we will like his characters. He is a good weaver of fiction seasoned with just a touch of humor. I think J. D. Austin is grooming himself for some very fine writing. He is quickly becoming the Yooper's answer to Tom Wolfe. Read him."

— Donald M. Hassler, Professor Emeritus of English,
Kent State University

"Although deep personal stresses and anxieties face the characters in these stories, there is an underlying sense of camaraderie and love that suggests hope. This a strong follow-up to the first novel of a promising young author."

— Jon C. Stott, author of *Paul Bunyan in Michigan*

What You Find in the Woods

and other stories

J. D. Austin

Modern History Press

Ann Arbor, MI

What You Find in the Woods: and Other Stories
Copyright © 2025 by J. D. Austin. All Rights Reserved.
Learn more at JDAustinStories.com

ISBN 979-8-89656-021-0 paperback   ISBN 979-8-89656-022-7 hardcover
ISBN 979-8-89656-023-4 eBook

Published by
Modern History Press   Phone 888-761-6268
5145 Pontiac Trail   Fax: 734-663-6861
Ann Arbor, MI 48105

www.ModernHistoryPress.com   info@ModernHistoryPress.com
Distributed by Ingram Group (USA, CAN, EU, UK, AU)

Author photo: Jake R. Bartz
Cover art: Ann Schaefer   Cover design: Doug West

"Free in Harbor" and "The Bottom of the Cider Barrel" originally published as written by August Whitney in *U.P. Reader Volume 7*.

"Steady Hands at Chicago General" originally published as written by August Whitney in *The Incandescent Review Issue 3*.

Library of Congress Cataloging-in-Publication Data

Names: Austin, J. D., 1999- author.
Title: What you find in the woods : and other stories / J D Austin.
Other titles: What you find in the woods (Compilation)
Description: Ann Arbor : Modern History Press, 2025. | Summary: "In these
  ten stories, J. D. Austin explores the nuances, pitfalls, failures, and
  redemptions of men and their families in the Upper Midwest. Locales
  include Chicago and Michigan's Upper Peninsula"-- Provided by
publisher.

Identifiers: LCCN 2025003358 (print) | LCCN 2025003359 (ebook) |
ISBN
  9798896560210 (paperback) | ISBN 9798896560227 (hardcover) | ISBN
  9798896560234 (epub)
Subjects: LCGFT: Short stories.
Classification: LCC PS3601.U859 W43 2025 (print) | LCC PS3601.U859
  (ebook)
LC record available at https://lccn.loc.gov/2025003358
LC ebook record available at https://lccn.loc.gov/2025003359

"Do you see that branch? It is dead but it still sways in the wind with the others. I think it would be like that with me. That if I died, I would still be part of life somehow."

— Anton Chekhov, *The Three Sisters*

"Everybody got dead homies."

— Mac Miller, *Diablo*

Contents

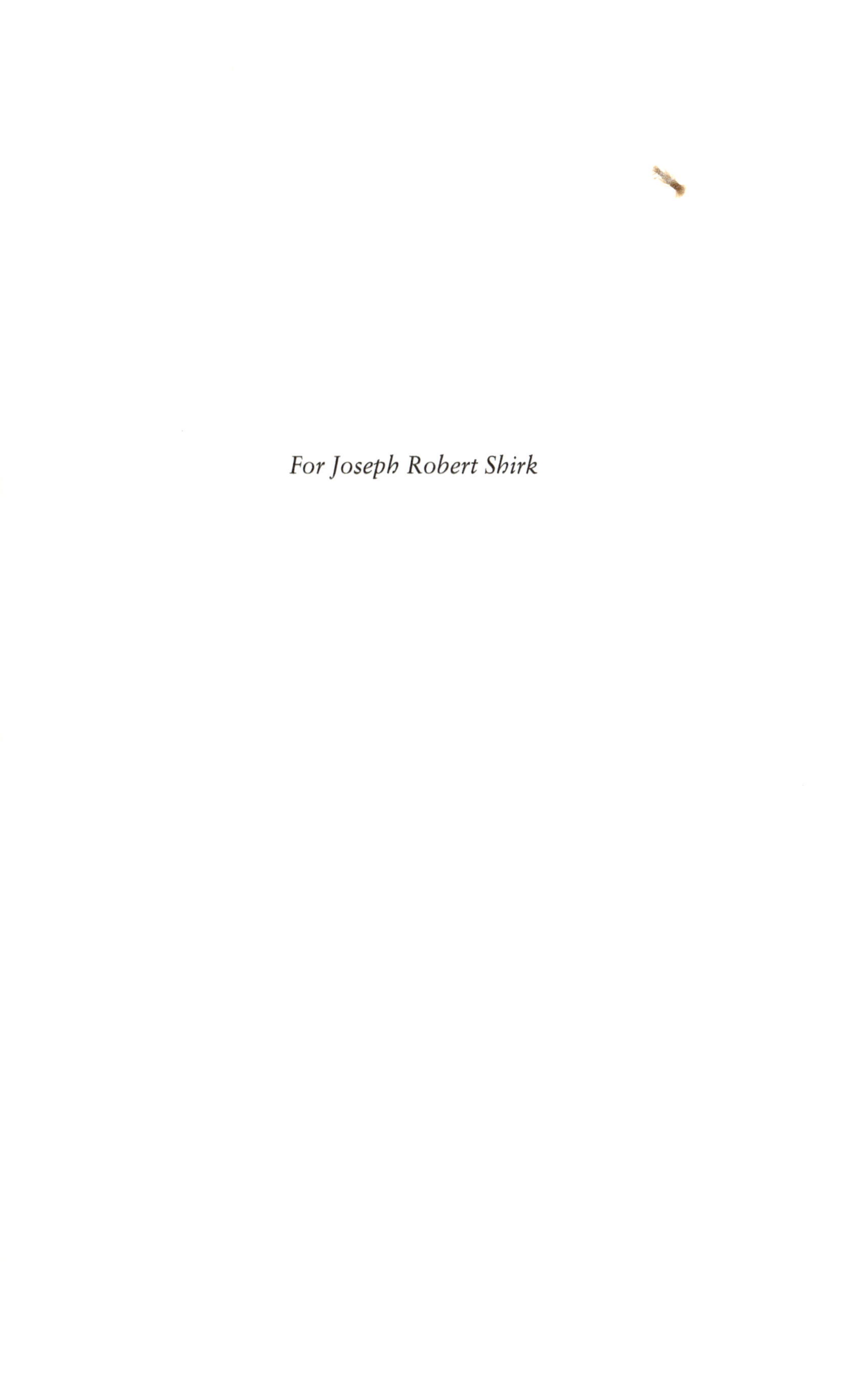

For Joseph Robert Shirk

The Bottom of the Cider Barrel

"What happened?" Roger asks, crouched over the hospital bed, wearing a control freak's look of frustration.

"Well, I don't know," you say. "I was tired. My back hurt. I dropped my pill case behind the toilet and gassed myself trying to pick them all up, I guess."

He rubs the baseball-sized tumor peeking out from under his shirt cuff. He starts to say something else but stops. It has all been said before. You're both frustrated with saying the things there are to say. He reaches out his good arm and rests it on your hip brace. He has tears in his eyes.

"Ellie, my love, I think we have to move out."

You nod. You reach out your good arm to rub his good arm. "Hey, hey. We made it. Honey. We're here. You're still here. Honey. What a life we've had! I remember it all! Don't you? Don't you remember?"

He smiles and coughs and wipes his nose. "Oh, I remember. But I don't...it's not—something spilled out along the way. You just aren't the same in my head." He starts to cry again. "It's been seventy years, Ellie. I'm hooked. You got me. I don't know what I'm going to do."

"Oh, Roger," you say, "We're not going to die tomorrow. Or, well, you won't." And just like that, as the wrong words like slippery fish pass from your lips and land in his eyes, you know he *must* be the one to die first.

* * *

They take you home on a Sunday. The maple tree in the front yard is a blazing orange and yellow; leaves crunch underfoot on the sidewalk. The swing bench on the front porch creaks when the wind kicks up. You can hear it from the couch where Roger deposited you. He's down in the basement, so out of sorts that he mercifully forgot to put on the Packer game.

On the way home from the hospital, you'd agreed to call your eldest daughter and give her launch authorization on the retirement facility in Marquette she'd been pushing for at least a year. Sons and in-laws would fill the place in a few days and empty it by the following weekend. And that would be that.

* * *

You met him in a rather unromantic way; you each were looking for a quick fix at the time. He made a joke about a doobie and you laughed, and that was pretty much it. When he brought in Tarot cards, he purportedly stole from the trinket shop on the corner, and asked you to read his palm, you nearly asked for his hand right then and there. Things were different back then; you were streaky and emotionally all over the place. For weeks you slept together and did a bad job acting too cool to really like each other. At the end of the summer, he was making pancakes when you had to run to the bathroom and weep. You told him you loved him. He said he loved you too, but not with the same gusto. It wouldn't be until later that he was really sure.

* * *

He'd decided to love you by the time you finished school. He came to your graduation and suffered through car rides with your family and friends. You went up to his dad's place on Keweenaw Bay for a weekend. The following week you left for a summer job in upstate New York. After a month, you were ready to quit. You called him in tears after getting screamed at in a meeting.

"My love, my love," he said. "Hey, hey, hey. You're so okay. Screw that guy, I mean, really, forget about him, but baby, baby, hear me on this one, I happen to know from experience. Getting yelled at is part of the job. I'm so sorry, baby."

"I know, I know. Ughhh. I hate that it affects me so much."

2

"Doesn't make it okay, but I just want you to know that this guy probably thinks that that interaction was ordinary. You're all good. All good, baby."

Later during the phone call, a roommate came in who was at the meeting. Roger asked the kid why he hadn't stuck up for you. The kid got righteous, at which point Roger got litigious, and after five minutes of going at it you were hysterical again, so the kid left. Roger realized he screwed up.

"Hey, baby, baby, I'm so sorry, I'm just trying to stick up for you! Hey, hey, it's okay. Ellie, Ellie, breathe for me," and so on and so forth for several hours. He was patient; he knew about your past, about what certain guys and family members had said and done.

You cried and cried. Not just that time—there were many instances, those days, of uncontrollable tears. Roger was solid as a rock through it all. Occasionally, he got frustrated, but most of the time, he was brilliant. "I'm like your sponge, baby. I'm here to soak up all the bad stuff. Let me soak it all up, baby. I'm here. I'm right here. I'm not going anywhere. I love you so much." And he meant it.

* * *

He wakes you up in the late afternoon, gently. He didn't actually wake you up; you heard him approach, hobbling up the basement steps and across the floorboards. You always let him wake you up, even if you're already awake. You're the snoozy one of the two of you. There has always been an element of flirtatious song and dance in his efforts to wake you from your naps. It was a sad day when, because of your busted hip, he could no longer wake you up by tickling you. And you had been sad about it, too! The devious gaslighting bastard. That's what you tell him, and he grins his gap-toothed grin and gently pokes your ribs through the blanket.

"I made you a grilled cheese," he says.

"Well, okay then," you sigh, and then you both laugh, and begin the odyssey of rising and limping to the kitchen; you lean on him, he leans on the furniture whose layout he knows so well. It was a minutes-long journey, plenty long to look at pictures resting on side tables and hung in frames on the walls, at trinkets from here and there, the detritus of half a century and more.

You know you hope the move will kill him; you just can't decide on whether or not you want to die too.

* * *

About fifteen years ago, you thought you had him beat. Unable to resist such offers, he took up a buddy on an invite to ride around the Great Lakes on the back of his massive Harley. It was early June. Roger wanted to camp, and you had to get a doctor to tell him, with you in the room as a witness, that he wasn't allowed to sleep on the ground anymore. He had some rather poetic things to say about it afterward, but you could tell he was devastated. Sleeping rough in the woods was one of his all-time favorite things. You heard him and his buddy (whose control of their own volume was inversely related to how cranked up they were) talking about doing it anyway. Apparently, there was some new fancy-schmancy blow-up pad that was meant for people with problems.

On the way out the door, he gave you an extra-long kiss. Later, in the emergency room in Thunder Bay, you wondered whether he'd anticipated the crash. An arm was mangled, and they had to do a bunch of skin grafts. Wounds got infected. He forgot to take certain crucial meds at seemingly crucial junctures. You knew you weren't ready then. And he pulled through, thank God.

* * *

On the flip side, you knew about his past, too. He was very open about it, and you loved him for that. About the hospitalizations, about the attempts, about the shrinks that drove him crazy with their patronization and their buttoned-up, sterile attempts to wade into his messy psyche. In the early days, he always said that you would get your turn. Part of his skill with hysteria came from his own father's skill with him; he was always quick to credit his father when you thanked him for caring for you so well during your episodes. He was brilliant when his own life was moving forward. But in the winters, he shut down and was useless in a crisis. He was always good at telling you he loved you. But in the winter, that was all he could do, and that wasn't enough, but it had to be.

* * *

"What did you put in this one?"

"Muenster, ched, red pepper flakes, minced garlic. The classic."

"It's incredible. I should eat up all the butter so you can't."

He smiled. "Perfect." He tried not to watch you screw up your features in pain as you swallowed. He tried to watch the shaking leaves in the rattling branches out the window. The weight of the half-empty glass shook your hand, and you had to bring your head down close to the table to drink. His fist clenched over a red cloth napkin. "I'm glad you're hungry today. I'll leave the other half just in case."

"You should eat it. Go ahead and eat it."

"Are you sure? I had plenty of turkey and rice for lunch. I should really not."

There was no reply.

"I'll leave it just in case."

"Thank you, darling." You put your shaking hand on his.

It would be crass, you've decided, to take the Lord's work into your hands and hasten his end. And you really should eat while you've got the appetite, painful though it is. You are only half-joking when you say you married him for his grilled cheeses.

* * *

The most romantic thing he ever said to you came in an insulting package. It was fifty years ago, your first or second winter, and you each were reading quite a bit. He was deep into a novel about a Confederate soldier hiking home across rural North Carolina. Some old man compliments a young man's choice of wife by saying, "It makes as much sense to marry a girl for her looks as it does to hunt a bird because you like the way it sings." Roger tried to dress it up by talking about your hourglass body, and he was right about that—still it stung, at the time. Now that your hip is broken along with your appetite, it's easier to understand what he meant. You are the type of lady who

5

learns. You are the type of lady who understands who needs to die first.

* * *

The following morning, your daughter and her husband arrive to start packing up. They're all gung-ho in a way that seems premeditated and vaguely sinister—Laura and her husband are acting like they have something to hide, or that they're getting away with something. Roger doesn't like it at all, and prickles. They won't let either of you touch a thing. You knew this and avoided the confrontation by sitting on the swing on the front porch. Roger joins you in a huff.

"It's like watching them divvy up your organs while they all still work. I almost flipped a table in there just now."

You rest a trembling hand on his knee. "We went through it all, remember? Everything we want is staying."

"Collecting dust in Laura's garage."

"Well yes, darling."

"A man shouldn't have to watch his own bookshelf get torn down."

"Hey, hey, hey. Shhh. Shh." You stroke his hair. "We can set up all the books just like they were in your new room. We'll do that first." This was apparently the wrong thing to say. He composes himself after a minute or two.

"Will they let us crash together?"

"I don't know."

"That alone might do me in."

"You're telling me, darling."

Roger sits bolt upright as if struck by lightning. He jostles the creaky swing as he hauls himself to his feet.

"What's up, baby?" you ask.

"My clubs. My...uhhuh." His breathing is labored. "My clubs. I need to check on my clubs."

"Aren't they going to Laura's, darling?"

"Like hell they are!" He turns and shuffles toward the front door. You swallow everything about not having a car, or someone to drive him, or a course close by to play, or a heart strong enough to do more than hit five or ten balls at the range anyway.

Roger always hated guys who took carts. "Just walk," he said venomously. "Are your legs broken?" There were scenes made with groups of younger guys who wished he would play faster. There were awkward insinuations from the guys who could still bear it to go out there with him. It was a control thing, and that only goes one direction with age.

You can hear him now, taking all this out on Laura's husband, who *is* a douche, and always took a cart, sure, but none of that was his fault any more than the color of his hair.

* * *

He talks Laura into leaving a sack of potatoes and a pan and some butter for one last dinner. She reminds him to be ready by eight for the drive on over to the facility tomorrow.

He puts on a B. B. King record when she leaves and turns it way down low, so as to not wake you from your afternoon nap. You wake up anyway and listen to him chopping potatoes, greasing the pan, frying them, spicing them, frying them some more. You hear him sneak a few for himself, even though the salt and the carbs and the butter will wreck his insides. He goes in the fridge and you hear the hiss-crack of a can of beer. He goes to the bathroom for several minutes while the potatoes burn.

You battle your way through a few bites for his sake; he blames himself for burning them, but the truth is that you wouldn't have eaten them if they were perfect. After dinner you both decide to get drunk. You sit together on the couch and listen to John Prine, and talk and talk and talk. You cry when he tells you about his beloved uncle; just before this man's death, Roger was talking to him on a late fall day out behind the farmhouse in his orchard. He quoted a Keats poem about a farmer at the end of October squeezing the last bits out of the bottom of his cider press, tasting the sweet sorrow in the last bits of light and warmth before winter comes and all is dark. The man was dead two weeks later, before the season's first snow flew.

When silence falls on the room, it's almost unbearable. You finish a bottle swig for swig, and he passes out on the couch. You fairly crawl into bed.

It turns into one of those nights where the minutes are hours long. Every time you think light is breaking in the east, the blackness just remains until you turn over. You hear Roger get up to piss. He joins you in bed, and for the rest of the eternal night gets up to piss every twenty minutes. You each nuzzle each other as you can but are rendered silent by the night. You aren't quite sure if you're having a lifelike dream or if you're just awake. Eventually your thoughts meander inward and then he's shaking your shoulder, the sun beaming savagely through the window and landing on the rumpled bedsheets.

He's waiting with his coffee and your glass of water. You suggest that you sit on the swing on the porch, and he agrees.

"Oh, baby," you sigh, slouching over to lean on him. "What are you thinking?"

He squints into the sunlight. The wind raises a wisp of white hair on his head; it settles in a goofy way. "I feel like a scared little boy on the first day of kindergarten. I want my books and my golf clubs." He says this last in a whiny voice and laughs at you, but you can see the twist of agony as his head turns every time a car growls around the corner.

"They might have a foosball table," you suggest.

"That's true. They might."

"I'll have to find a place to read in the sun. A nice chair."

"I'm worried about the food for you. I tried to tell them—the kid with the paperwork didn't seem like he was listening. I might have to get someone to do special grocery runs."

You give him your warmest, most radiant smile. "Thank you, darling. I'm sure it'll be fine. I'm sure they've had people like us before."

He coughs and starts to rise. "I'm just going to check the, uh, the basement. I'll be right back. Just make sure there isn't any, I mean, that we're all set. I mean, it's just…. I don't want to have to come back here once we're gone."

"Okay, darling."

You watch him hobble up the steps and into the house. As soon as he's gone, Laura's car pulls around the corner.

* * *

You married him for his brains, not his brawn, but in hindsight it was his instincts that were the most valuable. They were also cruelly on the money when it came to nutrition at the facility.

The food was crap. Barely even worth the Sisyphean effort of getting it down. They tried fluids, which your body promptly rejected. It wasn't just the foods; it was stage fright as well. It was like trying to eat in the cafeteria on your first day at a new school. By the end of the week, multiple major organs failed. The second day in the hospital, they moved you to full-time oxygen. On the morning of your third day, they asked if you wanted to speak with a priest.

"No, thank you."

Roger was there day and night. You slept most of the time. You told him about the whole priest thing. That afternoon, he left and snuck home, returning in an hour with a grilled cheese. You smelled it before he even had it out of his pocket. He gently nudged your shoulder to wake you, but of course you were already awake. You sniffed. He smirked and you smirked back. He handed you the sandwich and you took a bite. You hated the look of concern that sprouted on his face. He could tell you lacked the energy to properly chew it.

"I hope I didn't interrupt a good nap."

"No, my love; you're fine."

"How are you feeling?"

Your face screws itself up. "Oh, I.... Oh, oh, oh. I failed you, baby. I'm so sorry."

"What? What's up, baby? Hey, hey, hey, what's going on?"

You try to muster the energy to choke out what you mean. "I mean.... What are you going to do, baby?"

He smiled. "How do you mean?"

"Like, literally?"

A look of horror flashes across his eyes but disappears as quickly as it came. "Well, Ellie, I'll cross that bridge when I get to it."

"No, baby, no, I need more than that. I need...I need to know you'll be okay."

He looks at you with adoration across the blur of tears. "Of course I won't be okay, baby. I mean...I'm sorry, but things are going to be horrible. Don't make me think about that right now."

"No, please, Roger, listen. I fully intended to outlive you. Our whole lives, ever since we were twenty, up until last month. I mean, think, think with me, all the drugs and the motorcycle crash and the heart attack and.... it wasn't supposed to be like this! You were supposed to.... I'm sorry, my love. I'm so sorry. I'm sorry I can't be there for you all the way home."

He strokes your hair and wipes your eyes and says nothing for a good long while. He squeezes your hand tightly and kisses it at thirty-second intervals. Your hand, which had been kissed in an identical fashion for seventy years. "It's okay, my love," he says at long last. "It's all okay." And he sounds like he means it.

You calm down after a while, and it occurs to you to ask again. "Seriously, Roger. You must have thought about it. What are you going to do?"

You are immediately warmed by the glint in his eye. "What?" you demand, as his grin widens. He reaches out and squeezes your hand.

"Well, baby," he says, "I'm going to go on an adventure. Sam says he wants to drive to Duluth while the leaves are still pretty. From there I'll fly to New York where Leo Tyler's waiting with his boat. He's sailing to Sweden in November—"

"*Sweden?* In *November?*"

"Oh, sure, it'll be a blast. We'll stop off in Portugal and watch those knuckleheads who surf those hundred-foot waves. From there we'll head up to Scandinavia, where his wife is. That's the brilliant bit, right? I needed to get to Sweden and he was going anyway. There's a place up the coast from Stockholm where my father told me you could drop an unbaited hook and pull fish all day long, as many as you can eat. If I survive that long, I think I'll go see about that. If he wasn't exaggerating, I'll stay a while and eat fish all day. If he was, I'll head on over to Amsterdam. I'll get some kids in an alley to shoot me full of Jesus. And then I'll meet you wherever you're at."

You nod weakly. A transatlantic journey with the son of an old buddy in a small boat sounds like just the thing. If it didn't kill him, it would be the reason he survived. Your eyes close.

He strokes your hair and kisses your forehead and tells you he loves you over and over. Eventually all the sounds blend together—the buzz of the electric lights, the hums and the beeps of the infernal machines, the screech of gurney wheels on a freshly polished tile floor. It wasn't so hard to breathe after a while. You slept, and when you awoke you were ravenously hungry, and a young Roger was there snoring next to you and you realized, thank goodness, that you were dead.

Down the #5 Road

A fierce winter wind sent the windows screaming in agony—a screaming that used to be a cozy buffeting, but he'd gotten careless with the firewood in his first weeks here and the hearth had sat empty for ten days now, the raw wood of the cabin walls and ceiling lit by lamps and the fluorescents that bled in from the kitchen. Jake got up from the table and added his dishes to the pile in the sink. He shut off the awful kitchen light that reminded him of the hospital and stood listening for a second; he'd been haunted the entire month by a quiet rustling, a subtle knocking that he'd traced to the kitchen. His latest theory was that it had something to do with turning the light off since he'd often heard it, or thought he'd heard it, upon leaving the kitchen. He also thought he heard it at night, sleeping on the futon in the main room, when the kitchen light was always off. But he heard nothing now.

Jake ducked his athlete's frame through the doorway to the living room, flicking on a lamp on a side table as he did. The room sported Northwoods decor; tacky country home slogans on the sections of walls that didn't hold taxidermized game or posters of old Red Wings players. There was a green futon in couch form, a few chairs, side tables with lamps and magazines and coasters. He'd closed all the curtains two weeks ago when his parents left and hadn't opened them since. The night was just too much, and lately, the days had passed alternatively napping or on snowshoes in the forty acres of woods that surrounded the house. The curtains stayed closed all day; it was no longer a novelty to see a moose strolling through the front yard.

Jake sat down on the futon, set down his beer on the side table, and opened his laptop, his right hand massaging his right groin reflexively. His piece-of-shit laptop took forever to boot up. He got up and paced the room, checking every few seconds if the icon had stopped swirling. Outside, the late February gale blasted the windows. He had to plug his fingers in his ears as he paced. Finally it was finished booting up; he opened a browser and checked his email. It was a bountiful evening; there were two messages, not including the check-in message he got from his case worker (approval for his release from the facility to house-sit at this cabin had been contingent upon these check-ins). The first was from his mom.

Hey Bud,

Thinking of you as I am about to take crazy Daisy on this walk. We got a ton of snow in the Keweenaw last night, as I'm sure you did too. Hopefully Daisy tires herself out so I can get some grading done. It's not even March, and I'm already behind, and a lot of kids are sick, and I'm tired. What a mess!

How are you, dear one? Are you getting along okay at the cabin? How is your hip feeling? We've missed you since our Valentine's Day visit, though I had a message from Susan the other day—she and Don are having a perfectly lovely time in Florida and Don's lungs are truly much better off there, this time of year. They are so grateful to you for taking care of their place, and I'm grateful you've been able to get some time to yourself, though we miss you dearly. Don's certain you'll make a great coach; he mentions it in every message these days. How are you feeling? Is the medication helping? Lord knows there are plenty of bad meds. Just please don't do anything sudden with them.

I went on a walk with Lisa Peltola the other day—she told me that Conner Markham signed with the Maple Leafs! When I heard that my jaw almost dropped. It feels like last week that you two were little boys in the back of my car! But Lisa said the same thing, and the whole community is just so proud. They're having a whole party for him at the Downtowner for his first game, which is supposed to be next Thursday, in Ottawa. Dad is going to go with the Peltolas, but I told him I'd stay home—it'll be so noisy and all the drunks will bother me.

Daisy is barking up a storm so I'm going to take her around the block. I love you, Bud. Let me know how you are. We miss you, and we hope you are getting better. I want to message you more, and maybe call you, but we respect your wishes. Dad says peace and quiet in the woods will be a tonic after all that time cooped up in the hospital. Just know I am thinking of you every day, dear one.
Love,
Mom

Jake's pulse roared like a bass drum in his ears, the wind on the windows like a choir of tortured goats jumping off the walls of his skull. He gulped his beer and opened the second message. It was from Blake Rikkula, a high school friend who'd quit hockey for college and had fallen out of touch.

Jake,
Fuck me it's been a minute! I got your email address from your dad—I ran into him on Edwards Street, said this was the best way to reach you. He was hosing down the rink at the park as I was coming home from the grocery store. I was only home for a few days around the new year, but it was good to be back. I'm sorry I missed you—I heard you were home for a little while around Christmas. I have to say, what made me reach out is I saw on the news last night that the Leafs signed Conner. Holy shit! I immediately told everyone at the bar we'd played together all growing up. I'm sure you heard, but...wow. Two million a year, and a lot more soon. I mean, he was on the second line until senior year—you would know better. How was he in the U show? I was so jealous when you two went off to Green Bay after high school.

Speaking of which, your dad told me you got hurt last spring. I'm so sorry, man. That must suck so much.

What are you up to now? If you're looking for a job, my logistics firm in Detroit will definitely take you if I vouch. Just let me know. I miss you, man. I'm thinking about getting back into the game, maybe joining a men's league. It feels weird to say, but it also feels like forever since I played. You should come be my goalie when your hip heals up! Haha! Let me know what you're up to, man, and if you're ever in Detroit or in Houghton around the holidays, just shoot me a message. I'd love to get some drinks!

Your friend,

Blake Rikkula

He opened his message from his case worker just so he didn't have to reread Blake's.

Jake,

Daily check in. Let me know if the increased dosage causes any more problems. I looked into it and there's no documented heart-related side effect—what I did find was a side effect called akathisia, described as an intense anxiety and jitteriness that may be slightly alleviated by vigorous exercise. Would you say that reflects your experience during the episodes you described?

Let me know if there's anything else I can do. Be well.

Stacy Carrey, MD

In his required reply, Jake was expected to give a brief report of his day, indicating that he was sober and active, eating enough for his meds to take effect, and maintaining an acceptably buoyant mood.

He'd done all right in the beginning. The first two weeks before his parents visited, he'd risen promptly every morning and stoked up the fire, made coffee and eggs and toast, and listened to the radio. The coffee was completely circumstantial—he'd never touched it before his time at the cabin, but there was a big bag of it in the kitchen, and he wasn't supposed to get high on anything else (he'd scoured the cabinets and the basement for any forgotten painkiller or anxiety med the day he'd arrived, to no avail). He'd been afraid to drink coffee ever since he was sixteen, in his first year of tryout camps for junior teams. One morning, a motel where the players were staying didn't have any coffee. He played fine that day, but he was horrified to watch the sloppy play of his teammates all morning due to their lack of caffeine. In the locker room, everyone complained about it like they'd been deprived of a bed or a bathroom. That had been enough to keep him away from coffee, but four years later the circumstances had changed drastically, and in this place coffee was the only mind-altering substance at his disposal, at first. Then his parents came and dropped off his truck, taking pity on him for the weeks alone at the cabin. Four nights later, he drove the thirty-five miles to town for a thirty rack. His days had now assumed a regularity that he obviously could not detail in his daily check-in responses.

Jake had dragged himself off the futon in the morning at first light to piss and gulp a glass of water, and then another, from the kitchen sink. His pounding head and queasy stomach sent him outside for the sake of the shock. He tried to remember if he'd taken his meds the night before. The snowdrifts were eight feet high beside the door, but Lake Superior had frozen over so there wasn't daily snow anymore.

He massaged his groin and hip and stepped out into the dull gray arctic morning. The wind bit every bit of him that wasn't packaged up by his boxers; all six-foot-four, two-hundred-ten pounds that this time last year could've run the forty in under five seconds or snatched hundred-mile-an-hour pucks out of the air. His thoughts were already revving; he knew that if he didn't go back to sleep soon, equilibrium would be out of reach. He looked between the snowdrifts and out over the snowy field that stretched and rose gently into the distance. He gazed upon the hemlock, birch, and pine that frowned on either side of the field, forming a wide lane, and the long driveway that led to the county road. Everything was covered in four feet of snow, and the surface of the snow was crusty and frozen. Animal tracks had been easier to spot early in his stay—the snow was softer then, and still falling a few inches a day. Now the bare, raw winter bore down on him with cruel determination, and in the excitement of having his parents here he'd thoughtlessly burned nearly all the firewood, laughing with his dad about the abundance of the resource around him. The day he ran out, he'd found the chainsaw in the shed out back, but he couldn't get it started. That was the day he'd gone and bought the beer.

Walking back inside he paused, thinking he'd heard the knocking from inside the kitchen wall. He stood motionless, breathless, listening intently, only hearing the blood in his ears and feeling painful twists in his brain and stomach. *There it was again!* He rushed over and listened more closely. He thought he'd traced the sound to the portion of wall near the entrance, below the light switch. He put his ear to the wall. Silence. He waited. Walking back to the futon after a five-minute vigil, feeling stupid, he heard it again. The rustling, the knocking which he could barely hear, felt like a series of explosions that kept getting closer. The knocking stopped again. He waited a long while and realized he was now totally awake. He put on water for coffee and waited, massaging his groin again.

After coffee and a single piece of toast, Jake put on jeans and a hoodie and his thick coat. Outside, he strapped on a pair of wood and rawhide snowshoes. In the shed he found the twelve gauge where he'd left it the day before. He checked the supply of ammo. He'd burned through most of the buckshot and slugs without an animal to show for it, because he wasn't shooting at deer or moose or birds. He wouldn't know what to do with it, alone, anyway. Hunting season was hockey season growing up, and he'd always preferred the rink.

He stuffed two handfuls of slugs in his coat pocket and took the gun off the shelf and out of the shed. Trudging around to the back of the house, the snowshoes sinking a few inches below the crusty snow, he breathed in clean frigid air and drank in the color of tree bark in the snow. It was somehow brighter, he thought, and a lichen-type green sparkled from the bits that were visible through the white blanket of snow. It was quiet save for the crunch of each forward step.

He followed a rabbit trail up the hill beyond the backyard for ten minutes, down the back side, and then up again, until he arrived at his tree. It was an older red pine, forty-feet tall, whose trunk had buckled part way in a storm, and all that bound the bottom half to the top was a section of the trunk thick as a man's thigh, which held on despite being horribly twisted. The top half of the tree was leaning over on its neighbors, so the effect was of a half-felled tree that just needed encouragement to fall all the way. He'd found the shotgun during his frantic search for the chainsaw in the shed and had gotten this idea on a booze-fueled walk in the days after his parents' departure.

Jake fed a slug into the chamber and worked the pump. He turned the safety off and drew a bead on what looked like the most sensitive spot on the part of the tree that had buckled. The gun roared and punched his left shoulder; powdery snow on the tree exploded; the slug tore a dent in the part right where the trunk listed over its neighbors. But it didn't fall. He'd been doing this for four days now, and the tree had yet to give. He was going to run out of slugs.

Twenty slugs went quickly, and soon he was back in the warm cabin gulping a High Life on the couch with the radio turned to a station he liked that played the blues during the middle of weekdays. This was the best part of the day; he'd gotten up, he'd gone out, done some shooting, spent some time in the woods, worked up a sweat. He felt good. Each beer made him feel progressively better and turned down the volume. He'd never finished physical therapy all the way, and something about the snowshoeing aggravated his injury. He massaged it and opened another beer, feeling warm, feeling sleepy, his day-murdering nap now welcoming him like a seductress who has done her homework.

* * *

There is a peculiar horror to falling asleep on a northern winter morning and waking in the early dark to realize you have flushed the day away. The restlessness of dark when one expects light—it twists your mind and then lets it go springing back and forth. Jake had had some success recently waking before five and taking a long walk as dusk settled, but not tonight. Half again as many cans as usual sat guilty on the tabletops. This drove him to the fridge for bacon and eggs and toast, the meal he'd neglected to make himself after his shooting that morning. There was a moment of peace as he wolfed the food made delicious by his hunger. Then the wind began howling and the knocking started up again in the kitchen walls.

He stared at the empty text box on his laptop as the wind went quiet. He would reply to his case worker but waited to respond to Blake and to his mother. Several minutes passed. He typed for five minutes, deleting passages at times, reading it over after each adjustment, finally sending the message. It was a short tale of long walks and full meals, almost entirely fiction. But honestly, he thought to himself, how could anyone get through the days out here without a beer or two? He counted on his fingers: weeks since he'd seen his parents, more than a month since he'd seen another person besides the guy at the gas station....

All of a sudden, his coat was on and he rushed around the room, pockets loaded with joggling beers. His movements were jittery, knocking into the furniture as he gathered his wallet and keys. He ducked out the door and nearly wiped out on the slick front steps in his haste. The snow was gently coming down, a few new inches blanketing his truck. He got in and twisted the growling thing on, not waiting for it to warm up, and with a swipe of the wipers he took off down the driveway.

The county road, coarse from the winter's salt and slick with a layer of fresh powder, rushed beneath his frozen tires as his dark eyes strained against the blurry headlit darkness. Brights were useless in this weather—they lit up the falling snow and not much else. His bone-white grip upon the wheel looked ghostly in the glow of the dashboard lights. The first ten miles of the thirty-five-mile trip to town were out of signal range and had to be passed in deafening silence. The rattling of the truck made his teeth grind. He didn't see a soul until he turned onto 69 from County

D, the point after which he usually got a radio signal. He poked the dial.

"...chhhhhh dumps it rink-wide, picked up by Wilson who pulls up just over the blue line, drops it back to Johnson who rims it around the boards, picked up by Heller who goes d to d over to Rantanen, drive, save by Vanerchuk, rebound HE SCORES, A BEAUTIFUL REBOUND GOAL FROM BEN SCHILLING AS THE—" Plastic bits flew off in different directions as his fist connected with the dial. He threw two more painful punches for good measure, then looked up and swerved back into his own lane, spilling beer all over his lap. "Fuck!" Damningly, when he hit the busted radio dial, it stayed on. The announcer was going nuts over some junior who'd scored his thirtieth goal of the season. He spun the dial through all the country music and evangelism and found a high school basketball game. It was early in the first half and would hopefully get him all the way to the Copper King in Crystal Falls.

His gaze lingered in the mirror on a long straight stretch; lingered on his thick eyebrows and beard, lingered on his too-wide eyes and their whites around his dilated pupils, his nose and cheeks and forehead the raw red of gringos in the winter. The knees of his long legs knocked against the side of the footwell as his shoulders, hunched too high to be relaxed, twisted and flexed to find a position in which they could rest. He massaged his groin, which had been throbbing since he got in the car. He felt a twitching above his left eye, and he looked back at the road, white with salt and snow. His foot punched down on the gas as he took another couple of shots at the radio. The ball game went on, the volume undisturbed.

* * *

Twenty miles later, Jake spun out and nearly went into the ditch a mile or two from the Copper King. Shaken but stoked, as though the near miss signified preordained good luck this evening, he parked on the street and marched to the door of the bar and flung it open.

From the excitement of the last twenty miles, his lips stretched wide across his teeth in a rictus grin; he'd failed to consider that

21

it was, in fact, Saturday. The jukebox was blaring Luke Bryan as he shouldered his way through the crowd. It was two deep along the bar. The Red Wings game was on the TV, in the middle of the second period, the Wings down 2-1 to the St. Louis Blues. The bar was full of guys in camo and torn ballcaps, the same muddy boots they'd worn to work, not a single one clean-shaven.

Jake ordered a double Kessler neat and a High Life. He started a tab, gulped the liquor, shook his head and said, "Ahhh" with a gaping maw, and took his beer in hand to head to the pool table. Not two steps away from the bar, he felt a hand clasp his shoulder and wrench it around. His blood boiled, fists curled, stomach filled with tingly adrenaline. He turned, expecting an initial blow, but it was a kid no more than his own age, twenty-one, smiling and opening his arms for a hug.

"Snake! Jake the Fucking Snake! My boy! What the fuck, man? What are you doin' here?"

Jake accepted the hug with ferocity, wrapping the shorter man and pounding his back.

"I'm good, brother, I'm good. I'm just, you know…here to get fucked up, fuck some shit up, you know."

"Yeah, yeah you are. Come on. My boys are here. Come on." And he turned around and wedged his way through the thick bodies crowding the tables to their right and the bar to their left. They stopped at the last table where he was introduced to two scrawny guys, one with short brown hair, the other with flowing blond hair tied back in a bun. They wore muddy jeans and hoodies and boots, untied. Jake shed his jacket and shook their hands.

"This is Rick and Tyler. We clear brush together over in Sagola."

"Holy shit, no way. I'm near Sagola right now, and I'm losing my fucking mind."

The drum break from "In the Air Tonight" shot out of the speakers, and everything stopped; Jake was Phil Collins for a moment. He wasn't the only one, but his savage air drumming nearly decapitated a couple of patrons in the vicinity.

"Yeah, man," said the guy who'd recognized him. "Hey, you are wired to detonate. I wasn't gonna say anything, but…."

"Nah, man, I'm actually dead sober. That might be the problem. I've had a few beers, but that's all. The drive up was horrible. Blowing all over the road, and I couldn't see."

"Plows didn't get to 69 in time?"

Jake shook his head.

"We'll hit the bathroom in a second. I wanna play some darts."

Jake's heart soared at that news—not even ten minutes in and he'd nailed down a bump.

Another former teammate, and one whose work was near the cabin? He swigged his beer and looked over at the dart board—it was well busy. The pool table was occupied too, but no one was watching. Two guys were playing one on one. He took a quarter out of his pocket and set it on the edge of the table to set their place in line. His buddy, whose name was Syd, was talking to his friends. He grabbed Syd's shoulder.

"I got us up for pool."

"What the fuck? I said darts."

"There's a massive crowd around the dart board, dude. No chance."

Syd gave him a withering look and then shrugged. He finished his beer and got up to go to the bar. "You boys need?" he asked, pointing at each in turn.

"Shot?" Jake suggested.

"Fuck yeah."

They all crowded around the bar and did a shot of Kessler. Jake ordered another High Life and returned to their table. On the way, he jostled a petite woman in heavy makeup and cowboy boots. "Watch out, fuckhead," she barked at him. He nearly shot back, but his mind was on Syd's stash and a trip to the bathroom.

Back at the table, he gripped Syd's shoulder a little too brashly, even considering it was Saturday night and the Copper King was hot. "You wanna hit the bathroom?"

"In a minute. Before we play. Jesus, man, you are fucking vibrating. Have a drink, relax.

"What's up these days? What are you doing here?"

"Chilling, dude. I'm back in the U.P., which is nice."

"Yeah. I was surprised when you hit me up last spring for oxy. I thought you were going to play in college in, like, fucking Boston or something."

"Yeah, I uh…. That was the plan."

"So…what happened?"

Jake gulped the rest of his High Life. "I tore up my hip in Green Bay. They drafted a kid who was supposed to take some of the workload, but he was fucking Czech or something and there were visa problems, so he couldn't come over. So they got this kid who played varsity for a local high school and told me I'd be playing five out of six games. So I told them I'd need to practice less, that I'd already had an operation and couldn't practice four days a week and play every single game all weekend, plus morning skate, plus workouts—there was this awful goalie coach, dude. I mean, guy was stuck in the seventies, told us to play tough angles on our feet with our pads together like fucking Terry Sawchuk, absolutely hated RVH, made us do the skating drills with the outskaters in practice. I mean, fucking crazy fucker from the Stone Age.

"So I had to go in for another surgery before Christmas, and then a third when the second didn't heal right, and somehow, the third operation got infected. They gave me oxy after each surgery, and I always took like one and got rid of the rest because I didn't need them. The pain wasn't that bad. It was just after the third one I got the call from UMass, where I was committed, who told me they were pulling my roster spot. I kinda knew I was done at that point, that my hips were done. So I kept the oxy. That was last spring. I hit you up when I ran out."

Syd nodded, slowly, frowning with his eyebrows. "Holy fuck, man. Are you okay?"

"I mean, you know…I uh…I'm doing about as well as I thought, you know, given the circumstances. I miss it."

"Yeah. Yeah, I bet. Is this a bad time to bring up Conner Markham?"

"Hah, no. I mean yes, but you know, it's kinda coming at me from all angles, you hear what I'm saying, Syd? Like, I can barely skate. And people wonder if I've heard yet. My eyes work just fine. You know?"

Syd nodded, looking at him seriously. The pool table was nearly free; it was down to the last solid and stripe before the eight ball.

"What are you doing in Sagola?" Syd asked.

"Remember Coach Don?"

"From, like, mites?"

"Yeah."

"What about him? He must be ancient."

"Yeah, he is, and his lungs are shot." Jake gulped his beer. "My mom and his wife are close. They wanted to go down to Florida for the worst of the winter for his lungs, and they're having different people stay at their cabin while they're gone. My mom told them I'd do six weeks, and it feels like a THOUSAND FUCKING YEARS ALREADY...." He threw his head forward and then backward, and clutched at his skull, clawing down his shaggy brown hair.

"Hey, easy, easy, buddy; hey, holy fuck man. I think you need weed, not coke."

"Nah nah nah nah nah, weed gets my anxiety, man."

"All you goddamn goalies."

"Coke will put me to sleep at this point. Like Adderall with a kid who can't sit still."

"When's the last time you did any?"

"August, September. September."

Syd looked at him suspiciously.

"All right. But only a little." They walked single file to the bathroom in the back hallway. The bathroom was appropriately nasty, the walls plastered with ads for ice fishing tournaments and snowmobile events, promotionals for the bar. They went into the back stall. Jake kept jamming, pounding, the busted lock, trying to get it to sink. He bellowed.

"What the fuck. Shit!"

"I'm not giving you any if you don't calm down, brother."

"All right."

"We're fine."

He got out the bag and a key. He scooped up a bump's worth and hoovered it, tipping his head back. He passed the baggie to Jake, who did the same.

"Holy fuck that's good."

"You want a little more? Only a little."

"Yeah, yeah." He scooped up an equivalent amount and sniffed it up the other nostril. He tipped back his head and—he heard the angels singing for a moment. The bitter nasal fluid dripped into the back of his mouth. The speakers' music grew loud in his ears, the thumping bass and vocals vibrating with the beating of his sprinting heart. His pupils dilated—he heard the roar of springtime three months off—or perhaps that was the toilet flushing and Syd pulling him out of his trance in the corner. "Let's go, man, the pool table is gonna be open."

And it was. The guys who'd been playing each other were racking it up to play against Jake and Syd. Jake noticed a twenty-dollar bill that hadn't been there sitting on the side of the table. They glanced at each other. Syd asked, "You good for this? I got you back in a second; drinks wiped me out."

Jake nodded and laid down a twenty of his own. They sized up their opponents. One of them was short, bald, and hard-up looking; his shots were good, but he guzzled his drinks and stared at the table when he wasn't shooting, glancing every once in a while at the TV. His partner was a college kid with round glasses, in a T-shirt and jeans. The kid broke.

He sank a solid off the break in the left corner pocket. It was a good break; he had a clump of solids by the other corner pocket, which he clicked indiscriminately, knocking one in.

He missed his third shot.

Syd went first, and he was brilliant. He sank two tricky angled shots, the first ending in the middle right pocket, the second ending after a double ricochet, in the near left corner pocket.

The third he had to do a compound shot, which just barely sank without scratching. It was back to their opponents.

The short stubby guy sank two and missed his third by an inch. Jake took the cue from Syd and promptly scratched.

"Hey, what the fu—oh, you're good, man. You're all good. Hey, next round. We're warming up." This only made it worse.

The college kid sank two more, then scratched, and Syd nearly cleared the board for him and Jake. The short man made one and then missed. Jake lined up an easy tap in from across the table, got it all set just right, and somehow still missed. The college kid missed, and Syd sank the last one of their stripes. As the short stubby guy took the cue from his partner, he glanced at Syd and Jake and slurred, "We playin' eighballaspocket?"

"Huh?"

"We playing eight ball last pocket?"

"Fuck is that?"

"You gotta sink the eight ball in the last pocket you sank a ball."

"Hell no." This was Jake. "That'll take FOREVER."

"Hey, stop yelling, bro," said the college kid. Jake was way bigger than him and started to get in his face.

The man reached over and picked up his twenty-dollar bill.

"Hey, what the fuck, man?"

"This is bullshit," the short man belched out. "I been playing here fifteen years, play tournaments, you bet money, you play eight ball last pocket. That's how it goes or I'm not playing for money."

"You should've said that when we started! We're in a fucking bar, man; we're not playing some rule that'll clog up the table forever."

"Don't clog up the table, then," the kid chimed in. "It's part of the strategy, dumbfuck."

Jake had set his high school team's record on the forty-yard dash pushing a hundred pounds on the sled. With the same fluid motion and a rage-roar, he exploded forward and mowed down the scrawny kid who'd chirped him. The kid crumpled back into chairs, which clattered against the table, his head and neck snapping back as he fell. He pitched over to the side with his neck still bent, and stayed on the ground, motionless. Jake wound up and stomped on his crooked neck.

"Hey, HEY," Syd got in front of him, but Jake tossed him aside like he was a low-hanging branch in the woods. The bar noise was so loud that other people had barely noticed the skirmish. He went at the kid crumpled up on the ground. He kicked viciously at his kidneys and rained fists around his temples. The kid's glasses snapped and went flying. Jake wondered why the kid was limp like a ragdoll getting tossed around like a half-full punching bag. Syd was screaming in his ears when his hearing came back and the red went out of his vision.

"I think he broke his fucking neck, you fucking idiot, hey, HEY," and as Jake stood up, he saw that people had started to notice, and then Syd was steering him back through the bar and out the door into the blustery winter night.

* * *

The kids' partner, the short fat guy who was hammered, had followed them out and alerted the bartender when he came back inside. He'd watched to see which car the big kid had gotten into and remembered it even in his severely altered state.

"Kid was big, brown hair, bit of red in his beard. Talked like a hockey player. White Ford Ranger."

The bartender repeated this to the police, who scrambled the jets and had two cars on Jake's tail by the time he turned on to 69.

Jake drove recklessly around corners once he heard the sirens and saw the cherries and blueberries come flashing. He'd gotten out of town and was making his way back toward the state forest when he heard them. He jerked the wheel and turned down County D just as they came around the corner.

Car chases are better left to the movies, but Hollywood would have been proud of this one. Jake led the cops on a grand prix around the county roads. He spun out several times, but so did they. At last, he turned up an unplowed road at Johnson's Crossing, and for some reason, they just let him go.

The cops themselves had pointed him in this direction—"pointed" in the canine sense.

The road he took at Johnson's Crossing, the #5 Road, was a twenty-mile loop down through swamp and up into forest land owned by the logging companies; no way out except the way he came in. There were branches he could take, but all were dead ends, logging two-tracks that were out of the question this time of year. So the squad car stopped at the entrance and waited. If their man didn't show, a half-full tank would last them until backup came to relieve them.

* * *

The cabin of the truck grew quiet after the cops fell back—no more swearing, no more hyperventilating. The road bent ever so slightly to the left and the trees on either side, hemlocks and red pines, guided him against the sky and kept his wheels on the snow of the road. The snow had stopped falling; the wind had blown the clouds away, and now ghostly green banners waved and flickered up above, bright pale shadows licking the frozen snow. His hands began to relax—this far over the county line and no one else had come to chase him…maybe he was free and clear. Maybe the cops were tired or something.

The road continued to bend to the left, and he thought nothing of it. Remembering the beers in his pockets, he fished one out and twisted it open. The snowy trees were a blur in the headlights; he'd turned the brights on to find the road. Looking out the windshield into the sky, he noticed the shimmering green curtains and his mouth fell open. Right there, never clearer, waving like they're in the wind. The blur of the Milky Way edged in around the outside when the banners went dark, then disappeared when they flared up again, blazing green across the heavens. He kept his eyes glued to the sky even as he felt the wheels slipping, the brakes locking up, the truck sliding, grinding, pitching sideways, wobbling, and coming to rest ass down, nose out, in a snowdrift. He laughed and laughed when the truck stopped moving—the drive wheels were screwed, buried too deep in the fresh snow, but at least he wasn't nose down; his view of the strip of sky between the trees was unaffected.

He glanced down at the gas gauge—less than a quarter tank. The clock said 2:15 a.m. He opened another beer and yipped his head back to look at the sky, feeling comfortable, feeling sleepy.

* * *

The thermometer in the cop car said twenty-eight below. The two cops were listening to a sermon on the radio when their backup came around 4 a.m.

"Any sign of our boy?"

"Nada."

"You go get some rest."

"All right. Stay warm."

* * *

They dug Jake out the next morning when the sun came up around eight. A thin rime of frost stood out on his beard and brow. His shoulders were too hunched to have been relaxed, his smile too raw and sore. The gas had run out around five, and the wind was blowing. He shouldn't have listened to the radio or kept the heat on so long. He'd put on the evangelist station, wanting the sermon for company. It warmed up to fifteen below by the time they dragged his leaden body from the car, the last beer standing half-finished, half-frozen in the cupholder beside him.

Free in the Harbor

He was our friend, they said. And then they began to play.

* * *

Just before summer, I remember sitting in church on Easter Sunday in Houghton with Reginald and my dad. It was beautiful outside. I wept during the last hymn, especially given all the talk about bringing the dead back to life. Because for all the fancy spiritual philosophical mental gymnastics you can do to keep dead people alive in your head, it's just not the same when they're dead and you aren't. I hear them all in the music, the voices, and the organ, which is why it makes me sad sometimes. I'm not ready to die yet. But I miss my buddy Jim.

* * *

Today was the last day of the kayak season. As we haul boats in from the dock to the cellar, I look around—Greg, Terrence, Matt—and all I can think about is how little I remember. We've been sweating on this dock shoulder to shoulder since May, and all I can remember are the highlights, the greatest hits. If that's all they remembered about *me*, well—but before that thought sent me swirling, I caught a whiff of cigarette smoke and went to join Terrence, who was surely "checking the water levels," as we did, out back, "making sure they were safe."

* * *

There's some refuge taken in a common state of mind—at least *now* when we're smoking, we know for sure we are not alone. But somehow the process of calcifying this feeling into memory forces all its comfort to burn away, leaving only the foggy head and the dormant synapses that refuse to yield the mercy of a word, a detail, anything to remind you that they are real, or at least were at one point, and not just a story you heard somewhere.

* * *

Death surrounds anyone who is paying attention—then, of course, so do other things, but death should really be on the front burner.

Months ago I was getting on the Amtrak from Boston to Chicago. I walked through the dry sun out to the train and got on and sat down. A family with two little boys came in behind me. The boys each hugged an older couple who'd walked onto the train with them. The older couple then hugged the parents and left the train. The train rolled away from the station. The mother told the kids to sit down, stop horsing around. The kids sat and spoke in hushed tones. The younger of the two boys started to cry.

"What's wrong, buddy?" asked the father.

"I miss Grandpa and Grandma," sobbed the little boy. He cried harder as the father picked him up and wrapped him in a hug. "I miss them too, bud. I promise. They're coming out to Stillwater in two weeks though, remember? They're staying with us until Christmas."

The boy considered this between sniffles. "Okay. But, but what if something happens?"

The father had no answer. "We'll see them soon, bud. I'm sure of it."

The boy sobbed. I turned in my seat to face him. "Hey, bud. I miss my grandma too. I came out here to visit her, too."

"Oh really?" said the mom as the boy looked at me. I nodded and reached out to give the boy knuckles. His mom smiled and asked where I lived.

"Houghton, Michigan. I live with my father. My grandma's ninety-four, and they hadn't seen each other in a year or two. It might be her last time out to the Midwest, and..." I coughed and the mother tactfully handed me a tissue.

32

"I hear you," she said. "They always miss their grandma and grandpa real bad when we have to leave."

The little boy and I cried together. I thought of the coming weekend working kayaks in the harbor. I wondered if I could spare a night in Chicago on the way home. My buddy Tristan lives there with his parents in an apartment by the lake, and he's leaving for the Army at the end of the month. There's already a huge party planned, but I figured it'd be easier to say goodbye for five years if I saw him in Chicago a bunch first, when he's not in the middle of his last night of freedom, because lasts never count if you're aware of them as lasts. Or do they count doubly? Sometimes it's hard to tell, but increasingly, I believe it's the former.

* * *

I remember when I found out about Jim, the first thing I remembered was our conversation on the porch the weekend I visited two years ago. It was the end of a long night. He was wearing that bright purple tracksuit of his. We decided to head out to the porch and smoke a cigarette.

"There's this girl in my chem lab," he'd said. "I'm so close, man. So damn close."

"All right," I replied. "No more art majors?"

"Huh? No." I could tell he was confused.

"You know, like freshman year? The girl with the teal hair?"

"Oh, yeah. No, none of that."

"I hear ya."

Confusion played across his face. "Can I tell you something kinda personal?"

"Sure."

"I'm a, uh. I'm a virgin."

Long pause. "Wow," I said, wishing I had more time to calibrate an answer. "But what about the teal-haired girl? Or the one, what was that one? That was my favorite, man. The girl who banged her head on the wall and started crying! None of that happened?"

33

His face twisted up, and I wished I'd held my tongue. I was just surprised, since those stories he'd told us had such vivid detail.

"No, man. None of that happened."

"Well, shit! It's all good. Girl in your chem lab, right?"

"I suppose." But I'd embarrassed him, I could tell.

We smoked and things lightened up. He told me more about the girl in his chem lab, who he actually really liked apart from the likelihood of sleeping with her. Maybe that's what he'd meant by "so close"—not that he was so close to sleeping with her, but so close to feeling like he could, feeling like he cared about her, and in the right way. That was the last substantial conversation we ever had. When I got the news, my first thought was, *Damn, I wonder if he died a virgin?*

* * *

During Grandmother's week in Houghton, things were lovely and tense, as always. Reginald, our Nigerian asylum-seeking houseguest, was delighted to meet her after five years staying with my father, but he was also preoccupied with violence in his home country and threats to his family, from whom he was likely separated for life. He conducted this utterly serious business over FaceTime with various relatives in his blue penguin pajamas at all hours of the day.

One afternoon, I was out at the farm gathering properly sized sticks for the woodchipper, expecting Dad to roll up about half an hour before he did. I remember now—it wasn't a problem that he was late (because normally it would be, for me, emotionally) because I had fallen asleep with my back against a pine listening to the wind scrape over the tops of the trees. I walked up through the woods and then through the long grass to the driveway by the shed when I heard him pull up.

He got out and immediately wrapped me in a hug. I was grateful for this, but I also guessed that something was up. He said he was sorry for being so hard on me. I told him it was fine, he wasn't hard on me, which was true. We took our places on either side of the truck bed to talk—in my memory, he is wreathed in chokecherry leaves.

34

"I'm sorry, bud, I'm just a little…. I'm staring it in the face right now," my father said. "I was driving down the hill, you know, over by that McDonald's across from the Walmart at the top of the hill?"

"Yeah?"

"Well, there's this guy, he hitchhikes all the way over from Painesdale to that McDonald's every day apparently. I picked him up today. He was looking real uh…haggard. He didn't talk much, wouldn't give me anything but his name, Roy, and a few short answers. He told me he hitchhikes every day from his place in Painesdale to the McDonald's in Houghton for a cup of coffee. He was in Vietnam, judging by how old he was. There was fire in his eyes the whole time. I've seen him out there before and seen him inside the McDonald's too."

"So, every day he just hikes over, nurses a coffee all day, then hikes back?"

Dad swallowed hard. "I think that's all he can handle."

"Shit," I said. "I'm surprised he finds a ride every day."

"I thought the same thing. I asked him about that, actually. It's funny. He goes 'Yep, every day, 'cept Sunday when I go to church. Somebody always gets me. You just gotta be patient. Sometimes it's the first car, sometimes it's the hundredth. They always get me.'"

"Jeez."

"Anyway, let's get on these lingonberries. I've neglected their weeding for far too long."

And so, as the long summer sun sank slowly through the pine boughs that smothered our land, we crawled around on our knees, each with a trowel, attacking the weeds that had sprouted up over the last few months. I kept my eyes peeled for "runners"—little sprouts of lingonberry that spread between the larger bushes. They mature into full bushes themselves and spread their own runners, and eventually, the patch will all be one big bush.

As my hands dirtied and my nose grew accustomed to the rich odors of the forest and the orchard nearby, I thought of Dad's hitchhiker and what circumstances might have brought about his wayward mission to McDonald's and back six days a week. It reminded me of the previous winter when Dad had to tell me to stop offering Reginald rides to work at the grocery store, despite the icy roads and freezing temperatures.

"Think about it," he'd said. "Reginald is a patriarch. That's why his family is always on FaceTime with him all hours of the day. He's been gone from Nigeria a decade, and they're still on him every day for things. He told me once, I asked him, 'Reginald, wouldn't it be easier to just let them decide things for themselves back in Nigeria?' and he said, 'They would call me anywhere. They would call me no matter if I were on the *moon*.' So, he's the man, and being over here utterly reliant on us for shelter is probably pretty emasculating. His half-hour walk to work through the blizzard is the one alpha-male bit of toughness he gets in his life. Let him have it. It's all right. He understands the world differently. He's the one indefinitely separated from his family. He knows how to survive."

At the time, I felt bad for offending Reginald by offering, as though in the offering I had implied a lack of manhood, but I realize now that not offering would have been strange too. I remembered riding the bus in Milwaukee in June. In my imagination, my father's hitchhiker resembled in some respect a man I'd met on the bus, and walked a little way with afterwards, him talking, me listening. Or rather, I don't know whether they looked the same, but surely the shape of their warped hearts did.

* * *

About a month into the kayak season, I started listening to Stan Rogers again. The "first time" was all those years in the car with Dad crisscrossing the Midwest on the way to hockey tournaments. He and Mom were together then, and sometimes even kissed in church to trick me into thinking them happy. At first, it was merely nostalgic to play the old music I recognized, but then I branched out. Every morning, with songs of the old harbors stuck in my head, I unlocked the kayaks and ate my breakfast under the cottonwood tree behind the shipping container next to the boatyard. One song was about an old fishing village that had crumbled thanks to the massive trawlers who overfished and crowded out the traditional fishermen. The town was empty, the boats rotting on the shore, and every day, the whales swam free in the harbor, unbothered by the happenings of days gone by.

It was easy to project these songs onto my life. I'd sit on the dock and smell the stinky river in the morning, watch the seagulls over the harbor, and hear their cries. My life as a child had long since ended. No mom, no hockey, new city, possessed of only a far-flung group of buddies who were dying off one by one before their time. And here I am, just like Stan says, free in the harbor. Free, and crumbling under a desolation of the heart.

* * *

After church on that Easter Sunday, I was a wreck. Eventually, I ended up with Dad in his room. I was tearfully trying to say something about how once you know someone is gone and the memories attached to them are a different kind of valuable because they're all that's left, those very same memories become like sand in your hands on a windy day, slipping gracefully away in the tiniest pieces bit by bit, impossible to hold on to and even harder for the trying.

"I know, buddy," he said. "I know. It's hard, but we really all will end up in the same place. I was thinking about Huxley the other day...." He got up and pulled a pair of socks on. "Real quick—this is important, and I'd like to continue, but just for a second—you think a drive out to the farm might do you some good?"

"Sure. Yes."

"We don't have to do any chores. The woods might be soothing."

"You're right. Let's go."

On the way down the stairs, I remembered Brendan Huxley. I'd played hockey with him when we were both fifteen. He went to work at the local rink where my dad, when he wasn't teaching, was managing and driving the Zamboni. He worked with my dad for a year and a half, then turned up dead of an overdose at a friend's house. Apparently, there was some history of opiate abuse. He'd recently been kicked out of the house. All I could

37

remember was the kid who got bullied in the locker room, who couldn't make a breakout pass, who was nice to me but always managed to say the wrong thing.

Dad told me about Huxley's last days. How he'd fought with his dad about going to rehab. How he'd gone to live with a friend, only to come home when his parents called the friend's parents and withdrew their permission. How during their last shift together, my dad noticed that Huxley's boots were untied the whole time and his eyes remained out of focus and his hair was greasy from the lack of a shower. Sometimes Brendan just had greasy hair, but he'd always combed it anyway. The day of their last shift together, he barely even pushed it out of his eyes.

Apparently, it wasn't even suicide. Things got better before they got worse, and Brendan agreed to go to rehab the day after his last shift with my dad. He went two days without using. Then, the night before he started rehab, the urges took over. He tried to make a home-brewed concoction that allegedly worked like a "tide-me-over"—a little dose to imitate the good stuff he didn't have on hand. The evidence was inconclusive as to whether he screwed up the recipe or administered it wrong. He was dead within the hour, having destroyed his insides.

"That must have been unbelievably painful," I said, shocked, as we turned onto Coles Creek Road.

"Unimaginably painful. I remember his funeral. Everyone was in hockey jerseys. I spoke to his dad for a long time. I felt bad because he wanted to talk, you know; knew I'd been close with Brendan at the rink. He screwed things up a lot there toward the end of Brendan's life. I think he knew it, too, but he was just so...bewildered."

We sat with this for a minute. He pulled into the driveway at the farm, and we got out and stood facing each other over the truck bed, listening. Dad talked about how you never know; you just gotta keep answering the bell and trusting that things will not always be how they are right now. Easter Sunday is always a trigger, he said. Bringing the dead to life, even in the spiritual way of Jesus, was awfully tempting; the warmth of spiritual healing and love are so deceptively close to how it feels when they're actually alive, right in front of you, ugly and sad and wrong but at least *tangible,* something entirely outside of you, something capable of saving you, too, from the depths. Once they're gone, Jesus be damned, they're gone, and everlasting life exists on an entirely different plane than this one.

I had assumed Brendan died of an overdose. The actual details brought things strikingly into reality. He boiled his guts to death. Maybe not intentionally, like when Jim dropped a plugged-in toaster into a bathtub full of water. Not like that. But still fundamentally the same—grasping for something, anything, an escape from the way things are, the way life is. No, the way life *feels*.

* * *

Last Christmas, when the farm up the hill was under deep snow, my buddies came to stay in Houghton. In the winter, there's not much to do beyond skiing and snowshoeing, so we spent all afternoon having a massive snowball fight in Freda out on Lake Superior, using the bulging mounds and ridges of ice as cover. Red-faced and jubilant, we drove into town and settled in at the KBC. The talk shifted from the Bears woes at QB to a gruesome story from Pete about a cyst on his ass that burst during a piano recital. Tristan lamented his future sobriety and the lack of greasy food in the military—he'd decided on the Army but was waiting for medical waivers to process. When the lights flashed for "last call," we left.

We were all pretty greased up walking home up the steep hill of Bridge Street. We rounded the corner at the Seventh Day Adventist church, seeing the warmth of the attic lights beyond the steeple. We crunched up to the porch and bundled inside. We took off our coats and stamped our boots in a cluster by the door. I turned around at a creak on the stairs, and there was Reginald wearing a very serious expression.

"Reginald, hey!" said Tristan.

"Hello, you guys," said Reginald, his eyes cast down and aside.

"Hey, Reginald," I said.

"Hello. How are you all?"

"Oh, I'm great. We just got back from the KBC, which was excellent. We snowshoed around all day and explored that old crushing plant out in Freda, then had a snowball fight on the frozen lake. It was wonderful."

"Oh, yes. That is good."

"How are you, Reginald? How was work?"

Tristan and Pete had shed their heavy clothes and stood by politely at the foot of the stairs.

"Oh, well, it was good. I am upset because of the violence in my country. It's...." He trailed off.

"What happened?"

"Oh, I heard about this," said Pete. "Didn't Boko Haram just kidnap a bunch of Nigerian girls or something?"

Reginald's jaw set. "Yes, they kidnapped and murdered a lot of schoolgirls. Nigeria...I am at my wits' end for my country. The leadership, always there are kidnappings, the violence...I do not know what to do for my family...you here should know. You are lucky. You have so much."

"I hear you, Reginald."

"No, no. It is more than that." There was fire in his eyes now, and his voice rose with passion. "It is more than that. They take everything from you. When they kidnap you, kill you, they take everything. It's so bad, so, so bad in my country."

"I'm so sorry, Reginald."

"Ah, yes, well, for me I am okay, but in Nigeria." He shook his head and launched into a monologue.

"You must understand, you three, over here. You have your life. You have everything. Life in Nigeria is not given, and people are not free. I spend all I can keeping my family free, and for what? My countrymen go and kidnap and murder and...you, here, have your life. There are others who think over here you have much more than just your life, but they are wrong. They are *wrong*! That is all you ever have. In Nigeria, many have nothing, and those still in possession of their lives spend all their energy trying to retain it." He paused, looking at us with a boring, burning gaze. "*All you have is your life. And you have it.*" He looked down. "I am very upset about the situation in my country. I am, very...frustrated."

"Oh, Reginald. I hear you."

"Thank you, Reginald," said Tristan. We all felt a great gulf between us and him.

"No, it is good; thank you," said Reginald. "I am just...I wish one day to take you to my country when life is sacred again. I remember so many beautiful things.... Okay, I am going to go upstairs." And he turned around, in his blue penguin pajamas, and walked back up to his room, leaving us to ponder the possession of, if he was right, the only true thing that mattered.

* * *

When my train, which left the crying little boy and his family in Toledo, dropped me off in Chicago, Tristan was there to pick me up. Sitting outside Union Station, I tried to make time telescope so I could remember with specificity every single moment of our last visit before he left for the Army. His ship date was set for August 11. I was lost in thought when he pulled up to the curb, and I kicked myself for not savoring the anticipation of seeing him before he arrived, then immediately spaced out for the first few moments he was talking, forgot what he'd said, and panicking, suddenly felt like everything was slipping away all too quickly.

We zoomed north of the city to his beautiful apartment in Uptown, just past downtown. I hugged his mom and did my usual lap around their apartment to see the paintings—mostly French and Italian farmhouse/countryside/river-under-a-bridge type stuff they'd gotten from one or two artists they liked while abroad. There were some figures and abstract paintings, too, mostly cool tones, done by an uncle who lived in Virginia. After a few minutes, Tristan and I took the elevator to the roof and smoked. The view from his twenty-story roof was spectacular all around—the city to the south, layers of buildings fading into white in the distance on a sunny day, Lake Michigan a rich teal blue with little white triangles sailing to and from across it, to the west the El click-clacking its way north, like a model train from this height, planes soaring in out over the lake, headed over our heads to O'Hare. We went downstairs after a long while to watch TV and wait for our friend Cory to come by.

"God damn, do I love this couch," Tristan said, sinking back in front of the TV and wrapping himself in a blanket. I felt a pang of sympathy for him since he would be sweating his guts out in Oklahoma for basic training in two weeks, but he looked utterly unconcerned about that.

Cory showed up after a few minutes and we went to dinner. It was a jovial meal, telling stories about our mutual boys and asking after those we kept in poor touch with. Cory asked Tristan a zillion questions about the Army, and Tristan gave him a zillion-and-one answers. Beer glasses started to crowd out the table. There was a brief silence when the food came, and expressions of approval at it. We paid and left for Mickey's, Tristan's go-to dive bar around the corner. We started drinking heavily. I had the round of my life in darts, winning all three games of cricket. I barely remember the last one. We spent twenty minutes in front of Tristans's building saying goodbye. Back upstairs, we fell asleep on the couch in front of the TV.

I rose with the sun flashing bright on Lake Michigan, residual pink burning away, the water sparkling more and more until, way off in the distance, it was a pure reflection of the sun and sky. I pulled on my shoes and gathered my things. Usually, I felt awful at this point, like everything was slipping away and that I should've videotaped it or written it all down immediately. But as I walked over to Tristan's sleeping form on the couch by the window facing north, I didn't feel any of that. A bit sad, perhaps, but full, too. I nudged his shoulder.

"Mpfff."

"I love you, man. I'm taking off."

His eyes still shut, he offered a hand. I squeezed it twice and let it fall. He snorted and rolled over.

As my Greyhound bus rolled out of Chicago I wondered—why is it that before I always grew inconsolable when I left Chicago and my buddies, but now things are bearable? I thought about my last year and a half with Tristan. We'd left school, been unemployed, worked shitty jobs, and gotten each other through it. The Army was his ticket out of the cycle. Mine had been more subtle, with the advent of the kayak job. But here we both were, out from under the thing that we'd needed each other for. How many dinners had we shared, how many hugs from his parents, how many times had I walked into their apartment and known, *known*, that everything was going to be all right? And my stomach still turned from the whiskey he'd bought us, and my feet wore the socks I'd borrowed from his third dresser drawer, and though it ached with melancholy, my heart was still stretched to the max with all the kinds of things a heart is meant to hold.

* * *

One day in the middle of the summer at the height of my Stan Rogers phase, I decided to read his Wikipedia page. I was stunned to learn that he'd died young. I'd assumed he was either still alive or had lived his share; his music was rich with age. But his little plane had caught fire on the runway headed to a folk festival, and the entire flight suffocated from smoke inhalation. He was thirty-three, and I thought of my old friend Ricky who'd been killed in a skiing accident.

* * *

On the day of the first river roundup, I'd been thinking about Jim and Brendan and Ricky on the bus to work. It felt wrong to inhabit a world where all three hadn't made it past twenty when some of the people on the bus were either so fat or so destitute it was hard to imagine how they'd survived.

It was hot, and the event launched from the docks at five in the afternoon. A pontoon boat with a string band would play a few songs, then head north past the harbor to a riverside restaurant, then further north to another place, then down the river to a bar. My company rented kayaks to those who wanted to follow the band the whole way up the river and do a bar crawl. I got to paddle along as a chaperone to the boats people left on the docks as they went inside the bars to get drinks. It was a chaotic event, but the music was excellent, and the river cooled off in the evenings as the sun sank below the tops of the buildings. Once we were on the water, I was glad to be.

43

It happened suddenly. We were paddling between the first and second stop, the band trolling along slowly so that we could keep up. They were a bluegrass band. They took a drink after the third song was over, as we passed into the beginning of the heart of downtown. Speedboats wove in and out of the thick kayak traffic on the river. Along the bridges, people stopped to watch and listen. The front man paused to say a few words.

"Well, y'all, we appreciate you being here with us tonight. Music is one of those things that bends the rules of time and space. We need a little bit of that right now. This next one goes out to our dear buddy Ethan, who passed away recently. He played the fiddle for us. He did most of the work on this next song. He was our dear friend. This one's for Ethan."

And the fiddler's bow danced into the number, his fiddle moaning, and the rest of the boys joined one by one. It was a slower, sadder song. It was about being a little boy, catching minnows in the shallows of a lake with your friends, and then one day coming back and realizing you couldn't catch them anymore, that your hands had become too slow. And you keep going back and trying to catch minnows, if only to ratify the memory of catching hundreds as a boy. But you can't, and one day, you realize that catching minnows alone is impossible, and that all the little boys you used to catch them with are now men who don't care about catching minnows anymore.

Our Fathers

"Have you ever met a sage?" Louis asked bluntly, like the thought had just occurred to him.

"What do you mean?" I replied.

"Like, you know. Someone who is as close to nirvana as you can get while in this shitty world. A wise man on steroids."

"Oh, for sure. My dad. One hundred percent."

"You don't hate your dad?" He looked at me with surprise. We were at a stoplight.

"I love my dad more than anything in the world and it's not even close," I said. "He's the wisest man I know. Fiercely kind, adventurous, gentle, talked me out of killing myself twice. He's taught me how to live in the world, how to be a man, and not, like, the bullshit machismo man, but how to be the man I am, how to love God, and the earth, and my neighbors, and myself. He taught me to do real things, to love people, to have a project for the future. Those are the three rules. And he read to me until I was in high school, and still sometimes does. And he gives me hugs, and he fights pain and cruelty and sorrow with real love. Love is a verb, he always says. Love is an action. But he feels so much, and he taught me not to be afraid to feel what I feel, too."

"Damn, dude. I mean, that's good. That's real good," he said weakly, and turned to look out the window.

The light turned green. I gassed forward, glanced at the clock, prayed that we'd be to his place before 3 a.m. Louis's forehead rested drunkenly on the passenger window; the condensation surrounding the point of contact was lit up orange and red from the streetlights and brake lights. The next few streetlights were flashing yellows. I'd forgotten what they'd meant until he told me the other day when I was driving us home.

The buses stop running at midnight, and he's got a car, and he likes to get drunk after our shifts, and I don't anymore. We live a few blocks from each other.

That's how all this began.

* * *

Earlier that evening, he had told me he'd lost his keys. Not exactly lost—he said something along the line of, "Fucking SHIT, dude. I'm going to burn all my possessions and be homeless" by way of a greeting. We were dressed in black to work the concert, our long brown hair tied back in neat buns. I have a beard; his cheeks are clean. But people say we look like brothers, except for the eyes. I was taking IDs; he was taking tickets. I waited for the crowd to subside before I followed up.

"What's the deal, man?"

"I'm such a shitty mess. I was blacked out at High Dive, I guess, according to this girl I was with; she's thirty-six by the way, which is a bit old for me, and I did a bunch of her coke until she told me it was actually ketamine, and, but I guess I left my keys at the bar, 'cause she texted me that this morning. So I went back to High Dive, but they only had the fob piece. You know how car keys, some of 'em, have a fob attached to an actual key for the ignition?"

"Yeah," I nodded.

"Somehow my key part came detached from the fob part, and they only have the fob part.

"Thank God I left my car here last night," he said, shaking his head. "I'm going to call my parents in a bit. Actually, you mind if I go do that now?"

"Sure, go for it."

"Thanks, dude. Fuck me. I'm seriously going to burn my possessions and go to Alaska."

"Just go in the summer, yeah? That kid died. A pure, unencumbered soul can still freeze to death."

46

"Yeah," he slurred loudly, and I could tell he'd already started drinking, "but would you even care? Would it matter? To the truly unencumbered soul?"

"I suppose not, but that's not what life's for. The time of rest and redemption will come. While you're alive you can't help but be human, and your job as a human is to live and love in harmony, not detachment. Harmony will bring you to your natural end."

"I'd still rather they pull me out of the snowbank in the spring."

"Okay, but I'd miss you. Who else would take tickets and keep me company? No one else at this job will talk to me about books except you. People just talk about music."

"I'm sure you'd find somebody else. I'm sure you have plenty of smarter friends than me."

"Yeah, but they're not you, man. I'd miss you. Your job is to keep living your life, man, not to meditate until you freeze in Alaska."

"Doesn't that sound great, though?"

"Maybe in sixty years. I got shit to do in the meantime," I said, defiant. "And you do too."

"I'm sick of having shit to do. I want to be free."

I grinned. "Nobody's free until the day after they die, brother. We're all bound up together. There's only one universe."

He thought for a second. A few people came in and we took their IDs and tickets. "There might be more than one universe."

"Perhaps, but there's only one God."

"You believe in God?"

"The same way I believe in the sun and the moon, the snow in the winter and light in the summer."

"You religious?"

"Certainly. My Christianity has a Buddhist slant."

He grinned. "That's tight. I don't know. I kind of think everyone needs to come up with his own personal beliefs and religion, you know?"

"'A man can't have his own personal religion any more than he can have his own personal sun and moon.'"

"That your line?"

"I'm quoting an English critic named G. K. Chesterton."

"You're an asshole," he said, laughing. "I still wanna die in Alaska as soon as I can."

"My dad went to Alaska. He's got some stories from Alaska. Go call your folks and I'll tell 'em to you."

His face darkened. "Okay, yeah." He opened his phone with reluctant fingers and dead eyes. He got up from the table and walked away, out the door, plugging a finger in his ear as he waited for his parents to pick up.

* * *

Louis made me stop at a bar on Brady on the way home—Hosed, a small place decorated with firefighting equipment. There were two men at the end of the bar talking quietly and the bartender cleaning glasses. "What's up?" Louis said to the bar in general. He ordered two shots and did the second after I shook my head no. He cocked his head to the music, something off the White Album, and turned to the guys. "You guys playing this?" They looked at him and both nodded, immediately going back to their conversation. "Hell yeah, brother," Louis said to their backs.

I sipped on a cup of water and watched the clock turn to 2:51. It's an odd sensation being sober and hydrated at three in the morning, but it's certainly a good one. I just wish we didn't have to smoke it to the filter every single night, so to speak. I don't think I've gone to bed earlier than five-thirty on nights I drive home with Louis.

The song changed, a drastic mood shift. It was "Midnight City" by M83, a synth heavy pop anthem we all remembered. He wheeled on the two men.

"This you again?" he demanded.

The near fellow, in an unzipped black hoodie and black jeans, nodded.

"What, are you trying to get laid ten years ago? Holy Moses," Louis continued belligerently.

I stifled my laughter with a fist. I love when he gets drunk and gets in stranger's faces.

His Wisconsin accent gets thick and he says the most un-Midwestern things.

The two guys, however, were looking at us shiftily. Louis was closing out, the bartender shutting down. A Sonic commercial played on the TV. Louis turned to me. "You ever had Sonic?"

"Sure," I said. "Let's roll."

"I miss Sonic," he said, looking lost and forlorn in some memory. I had to jostle him to get him moving. I corralled him outside and back to the car as quickly as I could, and finally, we were headed for home.

* * *

"You gotta park on that—yeah, that side. You know, the one where all the cars are." Louis laughed at himself. I parked a few blocks south of his place.

"All right, cool. Shit, where's my phone?" He scrabbled around the seat and floor at his feet. "Gad DAMMIT, dood," he said, and I looked the other way to hide my laughter. The angrier he gets, the thicker his accent gets. I stared out onto the empty street, raw concrete bathed in orange streetlight. He ranted quietly to himself and found his phone after a ten-minute eternity. "Let's goh."

Louis walks fast; I hustled to catch up. "Shit dood," he said, swaying as he marched forward. "There's no way I'm going to remember where she is tomorrow."

"Your car?"

"Yeah."

"I will," I said. "You going to give me a ride home in the morning?"

"Sure. Remind me this time. I felt so bad when you told me you walked home."

"It's all good. I figured you'd forgotten."

He looked at me with pain in his eyes. "Do you think I forget all these late nights?"

"No, not all of them."

He nodded and looked away. The fact was he never remembered anything I said after we left the bar. I'd been getting better at covering my tracks and not reminding him of things he

49

was sure not to remember. I don't know why I said it so plainly just then. I guess it was late and I was sick of being up until 6 a.m. talking about things we won't even remember when the sun's up. I just can't bear the look on his face when I suggest we get to bed. It's like something's being put to death before his eyes.

He's got a nice place—wood floors, landscapes, and still lifes on the walls, a compact bookshelf. Best of all, no TV but an awesome amp and set of dials and pedals for his guitars. I played a little, but I figured out early in our friendship that he's too damn good for me to do anything but listen.

Louis cut up lines on the kitchen table. I shook my head no, and he did all four himself, successively. He grabbed a beer from the fridge and sat down at the table. I had a lemon La Croix, which was surprisingly delicious with the cold pizza we shared, eating silently with gusto as you do after a shift.

I felt a cat about my ankles, and another jumped up onto the table in greeting. Louis's got two cats: the white and fully grown, tailless Louis Junior, and the speckled black kitten Fanny. He picked up Fanny, who flailed about and resisted his caress.

"You wily bitch," he said, then tossed her to the ground. He patted Junior hard on the rump. Junior stuck his ass higher in the air; Louis cracked up. He's figured out that Junior likes the ass pats, but in my opinion he takes it a little far. He smacked that cat's ass hard, but the cat doesn't run away, so it's okay, I guess. "Rough around the edges," Louis said, with a chuckle. "Just like his daddy."

* * *

After the pizza we sat down on the couch in the living room and he played me a few of his songs.

They were pretty good folk tunes, all love songs but with interesting chords, many of which I didn't know. He played one about his ex-girlfriend, the love of his life to this day, he insists, and about how during the pandemic they were stuck in her parents' farmhouse together, and in the afternoons, she would make the most delicious tomato pie. I told him I liked it. He smiled, then frowned.

"You share your poems with your dad?"

"He's the first one I send things to. Usually, not always. Sometimes it's my buddies. But he reads everything I write as soon as I write it, yeah."

He shook his head. "I sent my dad that song, 'Tomato Pie,' like I texted it to him. He kinda blew me off."

"How do you mean?"

"He just kinda blew me off, didn't say much. I called him a jackass. You know, dude, it was the saddest thing. I called him a jackass and he called me up right away. In the middle of the day. I know he was at work. But he called me and was all bothered about me calling him a jackass, and I was like, dude, that's nothing compared to the shit you called me and my brothers and my mom all growing up. He said some of the meanest shit I've heard in my life to me and my brothers when we were little.

"And I sorta said that, on the phone, and he got all quiet, and then he just said, "I love you so much," and hung up. And I tried to call him back, but he wouldn't pick up. And I just felt so horrible because I knew he was really hurt. Like I know he's started to really regret a lot of things, not just being awful to me and my brothers, but that too. And so I was just sitting here, feeling like such a shit, like so low, dude. And then I got angry, you know?

"'Cause why am I feeling bad? I should feel good! I'm almost thirty years old, and I finally stood up to my dad. Not even stood up, just was honest about how much he hurt me for one little moment. But I know it made him feel—like, the way he said, 'I love you so much,' and immediately hung up the phone. And all of my anger and resentment about like, my whole childhood, suddenly turned to guilt and shame for making him feel bad. Fuck! Like, how am I supposed to feel? Why do I feel bad? Fuck! Do you know what I'm saying?"

"No man, I do, I do. I got buddies and relatives who I've had similar situations with. It hurts, no doubt."

* * *

An ambulance screamed by outside. The clock read nearly four-thirty. We looked at each other. "You think somebody's dead?"

51

"Probably not yet," he said. "Maybe they're close." He said it like he was jealous. "I'm telling you, dude, my advice is don't fuck it up. Take care of her, and don't fuckin' cheat on her."

"Oh, I know. I'm doing my best."

"I'm serious. Don't fuck it up."

"Doing everything I can."

He shook his head. "I know this is a ridiculous thing to say, but I feel hopeless. You know, about girls. She was—" and he rambled for a while about the ex he still loves. When he came to a halt and stared off into space, I spoke up.

"I hear you, man, I do. My parents split when I was twelve, and my dad remarried a few years ago. Never did I think I'd be saying this, but it's such a good thing. He was lonely and working so hard just to send me to college and camp in the summers, and I know he was depressed. He got back in the saddle, and because of it, he's so much better off. I mean, he's the most analog person I know; got rid of our TV for good when I was growing up, has a flip phone. But he met his second wife on a website. It took a huge leap of faith to make him compromise his principles like that, but in the end, real connection and love is worth it. People are meant to go through life two by two."

"Don't say that, dude. You're going to make me cry."

"All right," I said. "Well, I'll tell you one of mine. Before Meg, there was this girl, Sam. I wanted to marry her. We met in college and dated for three years afterward. She was super-outdoorsy, worked as a guide in the summers on top of her graphic design work.

"One summer, we decided to do the Appalachian Trail. Like, the whole thing. We planned it out real thoroughly, trained for it. I had things all set with switching from one job to the next when I got back. And so we went. Georgia to Maine. And my plan was to propose to her at the end; there's this incredible hike up a mountain, and I brought a ring along and everything. So we start off, and I'm telling you, it was incredible. After the volunteer shit I did in Africa, I honestly had such a low opinion of humanity, like, everyone over there was out to screw you over however they could. But the AT was totally different. People were incredibly generous, offering us food and places to crash, and friends to hike with. It totally restored my faith in humanity.

"But it was also just the quiet, dude. I mean, think—nothing but the birds and the wind in the trees and water on the rocks and the occasional voice of another person, eating ramen and granola every night for five months. It changes your brain chemistry, dude. It was incredible. But Sam started wigging out. She would, like, pick these stupid fights about really old stuff that I'd thought we'd sorted through, and got incredibly moody and we almost went home early because of it. Anyway, I figured out after a while that she had figured out I was going to propose. She had this major panic attack the week before we were supposed to head home.

"So I put my cards on the table and told her I'd planned on proposing but wouldn't if that was what was freaking her out, and she started crying even harder so I knew it was that. Anyway, we agreed that once we were back home she needed to see a therapist, and we'd wait to make any relational decisions until after that. So we finished up, beautiful final hike, and the next day we flew to New York to stay with my aunt for a few days. She lives on the Upper West Side. And it hit us, just the absolute worst culture shock or whatever it is, whatever happens when you spend five months in the woods mostly alone and then all of a sudden you're in Manhattan.

"That first night, you know what movie she took us to? It's kinda funny now, how ridiculous it is. *Transformers 4*. In 3D. In Manhattan. After we'd heard nothing but the birds and the breeze and slept on the ground for five months. Both Sam and I had our own separate panic attacks, and we had to leave the movie theater, and we spent the rest of our time in New York hiding in the bushes in the quietest corner of Central Park. We broke up two weeks after we got home. It was so hard, but she's better now, married to someone else. I can't for the life of me, even today, figure out what it was. It had to be me, somehow, the way she reacted, or acted, or whatever. But here we are, you know. Have to play the hand you're dealt, like my dad says."

A long moment passed. "Holy shit," Louis said. "I didn't know."

"It's all good. We work weddings and concerts, my boy. Plenty of beautiful women. You'll be all right."

Louis shook his head and went to the fridge and opened another beer. He looked back at me.

"What am I supposed to do?"

"About what?"

"Any of it?"

"Well, first—I'm going to walk to the gas station for a frozen pizza. It's four in the morning, and I need more food to take my meds, so we're going to cook that, eat it; I'm going to take my meds and go to sleep. It's five in the morning, Louis. 'Do the real thing in front of you.' Sleep. No more coke. We'll go for a jog tomorrow and sweat it all out. There's this great book, *Bright Lights, Big City*. The main character is this coke head who loses his job and his girlfriend and his life goes to shit, all because he wants so badly to be liked by everyone.

"At the end, just as he's starting to figure things out, he's all strung out walking home from a party as the early morning bakery deliveries are happening. He smells fresh rolls and walks up to the man unloading the truck and trades his new Ray Bans for a bag of burnt rolls, and the book ends as he's eating the rolls that're delicious even though they're burnt, and he's glad, 'cause he knows the trade was a good one, and the kind he needs to make with his whole life."

Louis swayed back and forth on his seat and grinned. "He trades his Ray Bans for bread?"

"Yeah. I'm going to run to the gas station now."

Suddenly he looked up, all wild eyed and terrified. "You're not leaving, right?"

"No. Just need some food to take my meds. I'll be back in four minutes. Just going to the BP on the corner."

"Oh. Okay."

"Just breathe, in the meantime. Just be still. Stay off that damn phone."

I walked over to the sink and filled a glass with water. From the freezer I threw in a few ice cubes. "Hey—drink this." I passed him the glass. He looked at it suspiciously, then gulped it down. I watched his Adam's apple rise once, twice, three times, four, and then the ice slid down onto his face. He snorted, laughing, and handed me back the glass.

"Holy shit, dude," he said. "That was incredible."

I filled his glass again. "It'll make the morning easier."

He drank it all again in one gulp. "That's the most delicious thing I've ever tasted." And he looked around, his eyes lingering on each new thing they fell upon, wonder playing across his face as though suddenly the veil had been lifted. He folded his arms and rested his head on them and closed his eyes, and fell asleep.

Steady Hands at Chicago General

Chris was waiting for Earl to find the clippers so I could give him a haircut. Sylvia stood next to me muttering to herself. It was my last day in the hospital after a week in the "Psychological Stabilization Unit." Earl, our favorite of the techs who took our blood pressure every morning, was bent over in a closet off to the left searching for the clippers. Chris needed a haircut badly, and I was going to give him one before I left with my dad in an hour or so. We had asked Earl about the cut this morning, and to our surprise, he'd said yes.

Earl was a big dude with glasses that always slid down his nose when he got all sweaty and worked up, which happened quite a bit. Yesterday was Wednesday, our favorite day because Sandy is the social worker who comes on Wednesdays, and she's the only one who will take you outside. The other social workers just look tired and say the game room (which consists of one ping-pong table in an unused conference room) is the only place we're allowed to exercise, and they send you to your room if you protest any further.

Anyway, yesterday Sandy was working and we played h.o.r.s.e. with a deflated basketball on this little stretch of patio outside. Chris and I were laughing all over the place because what else can you do when you taste the sweet fresh air after a week locked up inside? Earl was walking down the hall with his cart when he saw us frolicking through the window. He lumbered out, abandoning his cart. I caught a pass from Chris, pump-faked the jumper, and fed it to Earl at the top of the key. His shot went well wide, and he had to go back inside, but not before his glasses slipped off his nose. A well-practiced hand caught the glasses athletically against his breast, and he winked at me—"Looks like I still got it, ain't that something?"

* * *

It was 3 p.m. on Thursday now, and this morning they told me I was getting discharged sometime this afternoon. Earl was looking for the clippers and Chris was goofing off, but I was getting nervous because he'd been looking for a while with no luck. It seemed doubtful that Chris would ever get his haircut. Many things seem too good to be true, especially the prospect of being just hours or even minutes away from smelling the December slush that would soak my socks and give me blisters, but I wouldn't care because I was free.

My scrubs were filthy because I started tearing them into tiny little pieces at night, the bottoms especially. Early on I didn't know you could just ask for another pair if they got ripped, and I showed up to breakfast with a huge tear in my crotch. That was actually how Chris and I became friends. He cracked up and said something like, "Damn, y'all; looks like Kyle's got something for Show and Tell." I'd also torn up my one allotted sweater, and they told me I couldn't have my blanket out in the common area, so my options were freezing in front of *Law and Order* reruns on the grainy TV or listening to Tyrus, my poor roommate, scream through his nightly torment.

Tyrus and Sylvia make me very sad. They're going to be in places like this for the rest of their lives, but what people don't understand is that they're not as crazy as the doctors would like us to believe. They only fly off the handle when they're being hurt or ignored, and the nurses and techs push them into fits of psychosis on purpose because once the patient shows any signs of anger or frustration, the nurses just send them to their rooms. Chris was supposed to get out on Saturday, but since he's homeless and in the midst of a detox, his discharge is in conjunction with commitment to a facility and things got screwed up in the paperwork. He told me that his hustle is stealing books from the Salvation Army book drop and selling them for two dollars apiece at the gas station on the corner. He says it pays for

58

his dope and sometimes beer and food, too. That's how he said it—"sometimes beer and food, too."

* * *

After I started tearing up my scrubs into pieces, I began to notice everyone was tearing at something. Chris was tearing up the comic section of Saturday's *Tribune.* Old Artie in the corner was tearing up the color-by-number drawing of a ship he'd finished that looked nice but apparently wasn't to his taste. On Saturday, Sylvia tore out her bright pink hair.

She was a type-two psych ward patient. I'd gotten the two types from a story I'd read just before my first hospitalization. I've been committed twice now. Dave Wallace, via one of his characters in *Infinite Jest* said there are two types of psych ward patients. There are the ones who got dumped or lost a job or got caught up with the wrong crowd; they're full of self-pity and tend to wax on and end up in tears if you let them. And then there are the ones who are in so much pain that eternal oblivion feels like the only way to stop the bleeding in their suffocating minds. These people are on the roof of a tall building that's on fire, and their only options are jump to their death or get burned alive. The first time I was committed I was type one; the second time I was type two. Sylvia was type two as well.

* * *

Sylvia had been in for two nights when we were sitting in the awful plastic chairs near the nurse's desk that was lined with a thickly paneled glass barrier. On my second day, I jokingly asked why they needed to dress this place up like a bank or a jail and the nurse said, "For our protection," and I said "Aren't we the ones in need of protection?", and she looked at me askance and said "Do you need anything, Kyle?" and busied herself with computer work until I shut up. I was telling this to Sylvia in an aggrieved tone in an attempt to commiserate with her. The techs were refusing to give her her meds and her nicotine patches that evening and also refusing to explain why they were being withheld. She was sort of throwing a fit, and I looked up from my book and asked her what was wrong. She ranted to me and began tearing her frizzy pink hair out in chunks; then suddenly

59

she fell silent and caught her breath, looking around with wild eyes. She smiled when I started complaining right back. She seemed to be calming down, and so I continued to complain. I told her how even though it was hospital policy to let patients write down five phone numbers during intake so they could call out on the ward phone, they didn't let me get any during my intake, and when I inquired politely about it they stonewalled me for three days. I let my temper boil over and after that they didn't even acknowledge my inquiries about it, however delicate and sugary my delivery. Sylvia's eyes narrowed in sympathetic frustration.

I'm pretty good with Sylvia. She's hard to be with even as these things go, but I think I've pieced together her story. When she's really bad, she talks about this group called the Third Nation that kills people and uses their physical identities to disguise robots. She thought most of the nurses and techs were Third Nation robots with the identities of actual doctors who'd been murdered and replaced. On my last day she begged me to take her with me, to help her escape. They treated her horribly she said, plus she knew all about the horrible man who led the Third Nation and she could help me survive on the outside. I think she was talking about a man who had kidnapped her, which was what she said to me when she was most lucid, but her honeymoon with sanity was brief so I never found out for sure. When she was quite manic she would talk bitterly to Chris and me about how all the doctors wanted to do was kill the real versions of us and send out robot versions so we would stop causing problems.

"Psychological Stabilization Unit" is the official name for the fifth-floor psych ward, but it often felt like they were punishing us for needing help. The metaphorical parallels between Sylvia's hallucinations and the actual method of "healing" in the PSU were not lost on me. Chris said so in his own words. "It's the meds. I know for a fact. Last place I was in, they gave me Abilify for my bipolar. This place they give me Latuda. When I asked why, they said not to worry about it. I bugged the doctor about it, and he admitted that at this hospital they can't prescribe

Abilify because it's not FDA approved. So why the hell did they give it to me in the first place? Just don't make sense, man."

* * *

Chris and I were cracking up about something when Earl approached us with the clippers.

"Y'all fellas is lucky. I ain't seen these in years." He set the clippers on the table along with a fresh towel and a little barber's brush. Chris chuckled with glee. "Boy, you best get my hairline nice and crispy. If the ladies don't like me on the outside it's gonna be your fault!" He gave me an affectionate punch on the shoulder and then affected stiffness, adopting a snooty British accent. "I expect my trim to be sharp as a razor, little boy, and make it snappy!" He sat ramrod straight with an empty expression, but he burst out laughing after a few moments.

I tried to believe that Chris would be okay after I left. He was diagnosed bipolar like me and had been manically joyous for the last two days. Chris and I had stuck together for most of my week here. He'd already been in for ten days when I arrived. He didn't have anyone to talk to until I came and sat with him after he teased me about my ripped pants. I was desperate for company and he seemed hilarious, though apparently his jagged humor was too much for the other six patients who sat away from him, with each other in silence. Chris and I had sat together all week, and now I feared that my leaving would send him plummeting down from the crest to the trough of this current tidal wave of emotion. A lot was riding on this haircut. I couldn't very well leave Chris friendless and with a funky hairline.

Sylvia was smiling rarely over by the window. She pulled up a chair and watched as I draped Earl's towel over the front of Chris' shoulders and torso. I turned on the clippers. Their whiny buzz drew several people from their rooms, starved as we all were for something, anything, new. A nurse approached with a furrowed brow, but Earl intercepted her and explained that he'd authorized it. I ceremonially held up the clippers to the gathering audience, and Chris said a quick prayer, crossing himself sarcastically.

61

I started with a number two and worked my way around his surprisingly bumpy skull. His head and neck were cooperative as I gently moved him around to get the best angle. After the top was trimmed, I began lining him up in the back. Tyrus, my roommate, laughed like a child and with false terror told Chris that I'd mangled his hairline on the right side of his forehead. Chris slapped my calf and admonished me until I promised him I hadn't messed him up and that I would make sure his lineup was pristine. People were laughing now, more laughing than I had ever seen in my three total weeks in two different psych wards. I had to stop in the middle of the all-important horizontal stretch of forehead because I was doubled up. When I settled down, a nurse called my name and I turned around. Right behind her was my dad.

"Kyle? Your dad's here to pick you up. We've got the papers and your items right over this way." I looked at Chris, who rose and hugged me wordlessly, as did Sylvia. Chris sat back down, and I pressed the clippers into Sylvia's hands. It felt right that she'd be the one to manage the finishing touches. They wished me good luck, and then I turned and followed my dad out the door.

What You Find in the Woods

Thoroughly to Ana and Phoebe's chagrin, they were on their way to go ice fishing. Last night, the snow had fallen thickly enough that they'd needed to break out the snowshoes. The world was three shades of white; a slate of impenetrable cloud above, a blurry gash of trees far ahead, eight inches of fresh snow atop the lake, which had been frozen since Christmas. Snow squeaked and crunched underfoot, leaving five wide sets of treads leading fifty yards back to shore.

Jay, several paces ahead of the pack, stopped and set down his load. He unzipped the long bag and began setting up the shanty. Nick and Chris stood fighting shivers with clenched abdomens. Ana and Phoebe shivered noisily to communicate their mounting displeasure. They'd nearly decided to spend the day in town at the YMCA, which had a hot tub and sauna and, allegedly, according to Phoebe's research, a climbing wall. They'd agreed to come along fishing during the fever pitch of the previous night out, a decision that looked much different when the drink wore off and the sun rose on a frosty, gusty forest. Nick and Chris had been so excited, bubbling over with plans and talk of equipment and questions volleyed rapid-fire at Jay, who'd lived in Oneida County, Wisconsin, ever since he'd had a breakdown and dropped out of college, and among other things, ice fished every winter. The boys' sense of adventure had been contagious. And now here they were, blasted by the wind, standing around on a frozen lake watching Jay wrestle with the brightly colored canvas mess that was somehow supposed to keep them warm.

Nick offered to help, then a reluctant Chris. They managed to thread the poles on one half of the shanty, but the other required a stretching of the canvas around the second set of poles. It was excruciating to watch. At least eight times, Chris tried to yank the canvas taut enough to stretch the bent pole through the last canvas sleeve, and eight times he let go just a smidge too early and the canvas and pole sprung away from each other. Jay finally took over, running the pole farther at different places in the sleeve closer to the ground. He got the pole through its last section in two tries. Nick and Jay made quick work of the last few plastic snaps. The door was ceremoniously unzipped, and the girls filed in and planted their lawn chairs in the far corners. The boys went out and grabbed their chairs, returning to find that the shanty's listed capacity of four really meant only four. Jay graciously pitched his chair outside as Nick and Chris planted their chairs in the corners that flanked the shanty's zipped door. Jay returned with the drill and spade and fishing gear, which he handed to Nick. He zipped the door shut, took a knee in the snow, and looked around.

"See? It's not too bad when the wind is cut down." He tightened the long bit into the drill.

The girls exchanged a look.

"Could we start a fire?" Ana asked. "Once you get going?"

"Well, we'd have to unzip the door, for ventilation, for the smoke. And if it's hot enough and we stay out long enough, it could weaken the ice underneath us. Some guys bring propane space heaters out."

"And do you have one of those propane thingies?"

"I don't."

"Do you want one of my hand warmers?" Phoebe asked Ana.

"Actually yeah, thank you. I can't believe I thought I wouldn't need them. I pictured something cozier." Ana laughed a high, nervous laugh, and grew angry at Jay for taking it in stride, and angry at Nick and Chris for admiring Jay so much, and angry at Phoebe for clearly being the more agreeable girlfriend on this trip. The boys, Nick with his short brown beard and long mustache, Chris with his white-blonde two-day stubble, Jay with his gallant red beard, all had breath and snot crystallizing about their noses and mouths.

Ana had always been suspicious of vacations that involved work and neglected a nice hotel. She worked as an eyelash tech in Andersonville, commuting by car from her and Chris' apartment in River North. She'd never once taken the El. Her parents, given the choice, would go so far as to eliminate their last remaining time outside, which consisted of walking to and from their cars in the driveway. Ana's family lived in an old house in Wilmette whose garage only had space for two, and that space was spent on her father's vintage Jaguar and her mother's convertible Benz, which got driven three times a year between June and September.

Theirs was a family that wouldn't think of renting or buying if the space didn't have a fireplace, but only the kind, like Ana's mother once said, "That you turn on with a switch, and it stays behind a pane of glass so it doesn't stink or get too hot." Ana was tall and skinny and blonde and wore skinny jeans and brightly colored sneakers and had big brown eyes and a physique of the sort that used to appear more often in beer advertisements. She always had fresh lashes. They'd arrived at Jay's cabin on Dog Lake late the previous evening. They were up for the weekend on a kind of couples' retreat. Ana and Chris were college sweethearts (Michigan State); Nick and Phoebe had met at the climbing gym near their apartments in Lincoln Park. The two previous winters since Chris had passed the bar and moved back to Chicago, he and Nick had taken Ana and Phoebe to Arizona or Florida over MLK weekend.

Nick, Jay, and Chris had all played hockey together growing up, even together as a line their senior year of high school at New Trier. Nick had gotten back in touch with Jay for the first time in several years when Jay went down to Chicago for a friend's wedding the previous fall, and together they cooked up a plan for a winter visit to the lakeside cabin Jay occupied near Three Lakes. Nick's excitement had mounted to bursting as the date approached. He taught high school English in Chicago, which meant he read just enough novels to know that being cooped up in the city was bad for your imagination—that adventures happened when you went to the woods with your buddies with little to no agenda.

Ice fishing had sounded terrific when Jay had described it over a beer in Logan Square: sitting around drinking all day, letting nice fresh fish bite when they pleased. Deep down, Nick knew part of the true thrill of ice fishing was in its difficulty, but this is hard to really quantify unless you are actually out in shin-deep snow, warmed too little by the brief walk and faced with an afternoon of understimulation.

Jay cleared a patch and began to drill and fretted about his guests. He realized he had failed to account for some crucial details; while life at the cabin was constantly busy, with snow to shovel and food to cook and dishes to clean after the workday and wood to split for the stove that heated his cabin, he had no television. He used to have Wi-Fi, but had lapsed on payments one glorious summer and gotten used to it, and now he brought his old laptop to the library when he needed to check his email or look something up, which he rarely ever did. There was no cell phone service at the cabin.

* * *

His guests had been an hour late, slow to get going after work and stuck in the Thursday evening holiday weekend traffic. When Jay saw headlights flickering through the spindly winter branches beyond the driveway, he went out to the porch to greet them. The car sat running for a while. It shut off after a minute or two and everyone got out. Jay hugged Nick boisterously because he truly missed Nick; he hugged Chris warmly because he knew Chris didn't enjoy this kind of rugged vacation and so his presence was an honor; he hugged Ana politely with what he hoped was a misleadingly warm smile because he'd met her once and didn't like her; Phoebe he hugged quickly with a curt nod because he thought she was beautiful and she was looking right at him. She said, in a wonderfully boyish voice, "It's nice to finally meet you. Nick has told me so much. I'm stoked to be here."

"Me too. You climb, right?" She was shorter, with widely set dark green eyes and a button nose, vaguely elfin, in loose jeans and black boots and a dark green sweater with a light blue collar peeking out. She nodded and smiled.

"All right," said Jay, telling himself to snap out of it. "Why don't you guys grab your bags and get set up?"

Nick and Phoebe got the room upstairs, while Chris and Ana headed for the basement.

Jay was accustomed to bundling up for the sake of saving wood, and he realized as he watched the two city couples shiver that the place was rather cold. He poked the coals around and added the thickest pieces from the cardboard box beside the stove. The fire had died down more than he realized, so he added twigs from the basket of kindling, and a snapping and popping announced flames that grew quickly.

Soon the couples joined him around the stove. Jay looked around nervously. "Everything should be all ready for you guys—blankets and towels and all that. Let me know if you need more. I'll feed the fire a bunch before we go out so the place is nice and warm when we get back."

Chris and Nick nodded their thanks. Ana looked at Jay. "Could we turn on the thermostat downstairs? It was really freezing in our room just now."

Jay looked at Chris and chuckled at the joke. The sirens in Chris' eyes warned him of his mistake. "What's funny?" Ana asked acidly. "I don't get it."

Jay took a breath and put another piece of wood on the fire and tried to pick his words diplomatically. "This woodstove heats the house up," he said. "I'll chop some extra wood tomorrow morning so we can keep the place toasty all weekend."

"Okay," said Ana. "But why not just turn on the heat?"

Jay looked patiently at Ana and said, in his calmest voice, "I heat the place with this stove." Her mouth had opened before Jay was even finished. Her jaw hung there for a second like a drop of water clinging to the rim of a faucet before shutting quickly and setting hard.

"Do you need us to chop more wood?" Nick asked, trying to be helpful and hoping that was the right question.

Jay shook his head. "You guys are hungry I bet. We have enough to burn as much as we want tonight. I'll split more in the morning. I'm about ready to sit in one place and eat and drink for a while. What do you guys think?"

"Yeah, sure!" said Phoebe and Nick in unison. Chris nodded and Ana shrugged.

"All right," said Jay, and he put another two pieces on the fire. Ana suggested the boys sit in the back of Phoebe's sedan so that the girls wouldn't have to squeeze. The whole way over to the bar in the back they poked and tickled and punched each other, giddily telling stories and laughing harder than they ought to the way boys do who love each other lots and haven't been all together in a while. Ana told them to knock it off twice, the second time snapping back at them after Phoebe lurched forward when, in the course of their roughhousing, they bumped into the back of the driver's seat.

Nick, who unbeknownst to Jay also detested Ana, could see a rather dangerous dynamic developing. Ana kept doing an "us-and-them" thing, pitting her and Phoebe against the boys. She'd done it already several times on the drive up. Nick could tell it was getting to Phoebe, who was in her second of four years finishing a chemistry PhD at Loyola and who regularly got hurt proving herself just as tough as any other guy in the climbing gym. Later, when ice fishing came up at the bar and the boys, two drinks ahead, were much more excited than she and Ana, Jay noticed and suggested the YMCA, secretly hoping they would take the bait and fuck off for a day so the boys could have a good day fishing.

The infuriating thing for Phoebe was she actually did want to climb and sit in the hot tub and relax all day. That was *exactly* what she wanted. But after sensing the condescension buried deeply in her host's roughened, wrinkled dark brown eyes, and after listening to Ana talk the whole way up about "girls' time" and "what would be good for the girls," and after thinking about it over the course of a second and then a third beer, she decided hell would freeze over before she spend a whole day alone with the chattery Ana so the men could have adventures in peace.

Phoebe shoved her gloved hands deeper into her coat pockets and avoided Ana's eye as Jay drilled into the ice. She couldn't believe he wasn't wearing gloves. Her fingers felt like icicles ready to snap if they got any colder. Everyone except Jay flinched when his drill finally broke through and he drew it up quickly, splashing out shards of frozen lake and bits of water that stung as though they were boiling. Quickly, Jay baited a hook and dropped the line and set it, examining its sturdiness and finally looking up and around, as if just now realizing that everyone was still there with him. Because she couldn't bear the silence, Phoebe thought of a question.

"So, you do this every winter?" she asked Jay as he opened a backpack and passed out bottles of Labatt's.

He looked up and nodded. "Usually twice a week after the freeze, as long as I have buddies to go with. It's not much fun out here without company. A good season will last three months."

Nick was shaking his head and smiling. "That's so goddamn cool," he gushed. Jay looked at him a bit confused as he went on. "I mean, I live on the lake in Chicago, and I still consider it a good week if I go for a walk once a week. A walk. Do you ever go out and not catch anything?"

"About half the time. It's okay, though. It's nice to see the guys I fish with, and the days where we get a bunch make it all worth it."

"So cool," said Nick, shaking his head. "So goddamn cool. I wish I had just one friend, besides you obviously, who was that cool. You're the only guy I know who I could call up to run around with in the woods in the winter."

Jay was a little bewildered, but smiled graciously. "Well, hell. I appreciate that." He looked down at the hole in the ice. "Not much else to do in the winter up here."

"I love fresh fish," said Ana, and everybody nodded and sipped their beers, glad that warmth and agreement were seeping back into their bones. "I had—guys, remember that lobster we all had in Fort Lauderdale last year?" She paused and looked at Phoebe and Chris and Nick. Chris smiled and Phoebe nodded.

"Oh my God….so soft, they told us they get it all fresh every morning. We went for lunch, so it must've come out of the water barely hours before we ate it. Apparently Guy Fieri has gone there. He likes it, apparently. They had this butter sauce…. Have you ever had lobster, Jay? They don't have that up here, do they?" He shook his head no. "But I've had it in Florida before," he said a little defensively. "I used to go down to the Keys every spring for spearfishing. Lobster's great."

"Oh, the Keys are so trashy, though," said Ana.

"There's incredible fishing there," said Nick defensively. "Not as much tourism. Anyway, ocean fishing and fishing the streams and lakes up here is different, right?" Nick again looked at Jay, hoping again to be right.

"I suppose, yeah," said Jay, who was still trying to figure out whether Nick was on a sarcastic jag or what. Last night at the bar Nick's exclamations about how cheap everything was had drawn looks from locals that Jay recognized. Nick was the kind of guy from Chicago that thought that growing a long beard and packing a suitcase full of flannel and denim would make him just like anyone else in the rural north. He knew Nick was smart, but he didn't think that he was cruel. He was just inordinately romantic about a thing he didn't really understand. Jay looked at the line for something to do, tugging at it experimentally.

"You ever get anything real big?" Chris asked. Finally, the right question. Jay tee'd up the one he told most often in the bar.

"Well, nothing too huge myself. Got some nice trout up here at a few of my spots, but they aren't shit to what's in the ocean, like Nick said. But there was one time," said Jay, warming up. "One time I went out with a fella I met spear fishing in the Keys; we got to talking one night at the bar, and in the course of conversation, I told him I tie flies and sell 'em online. He pulls out his phone and looks at my website and practically has a seizure when he sees 'em. Guy from Atlanta, real nice, but, you know, I'd seen his watch, I know he's got some money. He starts asking me if he can buy my whole inventory. Everything I got, plus new orders. I tell him, 'Hey, sure, but I run a forklift at the lumberyard five days a week so it'll take a while.'

"He says no problem. He invites me out the next day to dive and spearfish way the hell out there on his swanky new boat. So I say, 'Sure, of course,' and he texted me directions to his slip right there at the bar. So I show up the next morning, early like he said, half-expecting it to be a joke, you know, 'cause if he really ended up buying all my flies, that's, like, a couple thousand maybe. But it's no joke. The boat itself was kind of ugly, too modern and kind of snub-nosed, but I could tell right away it cost a shit-ton. Massive engines and polished wood and all that. He saw me right away and came out of the cabin, fresh like we hadn't been drinking together five hours before. So we go out, and he gets me all suited up with diving equipment and tells me he'll hand me the spear gun if we run into anything big.

"Now we're way the hell out there, can barely see the buildings on shore. We dive together and go down a little, and the water is this bright turquoise, and right away this massive tuna comes drifting by like twenty yards in front of us. He looked at me with huge eyes and handed me the gun slowly. I couldn't believe it. I got it right behind the head. He hugged me right there in the water. Thing was five feet long and musclebound. We hauled it up, and he said I could have it to sell or for the meat if I agreed to sell him all my inventory at the time. I mean, that's a five- or six-thousand-dollar fish, plus a massive fly order—"

"Hold on, why five or six thousand?" Phoebe asked.

"Because that's what he thought it would go for on the open market. I mean, I'm not as much in that world, but it was a huge fucking fish. Lots of meat. I think it'd be at least a couple grand."

Chris and Nick were shaking their heads. "Incredible. That is just fucking incredible," they were saying.

"So," Phoebe asked, "what did you do with it?"

"I had it butchered, sold about half, and froze the other half. I finished it last summer."

"What'd you get for what you sold?"

"A bit over a grand, and the flies came out to about four grand. I got myself a shotgun and saved the rest."

It took everyone a second to realize he was dead serious. "Well," Ana said.

"Incredible," Nick said again. "That's the way life really oughta be. Adventuring and coming back rich. Incredible." He shook his head. Phoebe looked at Jay, who looked away and then checked back sheepishly, and then looked away for good. She hoped her subtle flirting would make up for Nick's unwittingly condescending fawning over his friend's life.

"Can you pass me another beer?" she asked.

The conversation puttered along in second gear about fish prices and turkey hunting and stream access laws until Ana took over with an anecdote about a client. This was met with long gulps of beer from the boys, until Phoebe gave a little cry and said, "Hey, hey, Jay, I think we got something."

Jay pulled up the line, and sure enough, a slimy wriggling perch, strangely bulbous, came flapping from the hole in the ice. Ana gave a little scream as Jay cut the line and looked around with a grin.

"Well, how about it! This one's thick for some reason!" He turned to Nick with mischief in his eyes. "Want a kiss?" And he shoved the wet fish in Nick's face. Nick recoiled, then went in for a terrified peck.

Chris shook his head no when offered. "What do we do now?" he asked.

"I'll kill it, and then we can either keep fishing or go in and cook it and warm up."

"How are you going to kill it?" asked Ana.

"I'll probably slam it on some packed snow. Usually we bring a mallet or something."

"That's so mean," Ana scolded. "Wouldn't it just die if you left it out in the snow?"

"I don't know. You're supposed to kill them quickly."

She just shook her head. "Just put it out in the snow. I'll throw up if you beat it to death."

Jay looked around at everyone else for some common sense, and everyone else avoided his eyes. Neutrality was the solution when it came to getting along with Ana. Jay shrugged and unzipped the shanty and nestled the squirming fish in the snow outside. He felt bad for it, but it was only Friday, and he knew he'd regret it if he pissed anyone's girlfriend off this early in the weekend.

They quickly agreed that they'd all had enough fishing and were ready to go in and cook it up and get ready for the evening. They'd been out for a couple of hours, after all. Everyone filed out of the shanty clutching their lawn chair. Jay broke down the operation. The world was still a globe of white and gray, perhaps a little darker, but essentially the same. It felt good to stretch their legs on the walk back to shore and the climb up the hill to Jay's place. Only once they were inside did Jay realize they'd forgotten their catch out in the snow.

"We'll come with," said Nick, grabbing Phoebe's hand as Jay headed back out the door.

They trudged back out to the lake in silence. It was palpably darker and snow was falling gently, making it hard to see across to the trees on the opposite shore. Jay hunted around in the snow, coming up seconds later with the fat fish still squirming, though weakly, certainly conscious of its own defeat. He looked pissed.

"I knew I should've just killed it right away." He looked at Nick and Phoebe apologetically. They shook their heads. He stomped down a section of snow and began to raise the fish over his head, holding it by the tail, until Phoebe reached out.

"Wait."

He stopped. "What's up?"

"Can I?"

Jay looked at Nick for reassurance, which made Phoebe certain she wanted what she wanted. "Let me." Jay handed over the fish.

Phoebe raised it high and brought it down like a hammer with a soft, underwhelming thud. She followed the first up with two more in rapid succession, holding out the fish afterward to see if any life was left. It hung in her hand like a fat, wet rope. Nick looked a little pale. Phoebe looked around and marched back toward the cabin, and the boys, exchanging rather shocked glances, shrugged and followed her back. Jay felt a blackness coming over him, from a place he couldn't quite identify, beyond the fact that he was aiding and abetting the exact kind of tourism his ice-fishing buddies railed against. He should've just killed the fish right away. Back inside, Ana was already in her pink fuzzy socks. "Was it dead?" she asked, eyes glued to Phoebe's back as she set the dead fish on the countertop.

"No. It is now." Jay hung up his coat and began looking for a knife.

"What did you do to it?"

"Me? Nothing."

Ana wheeled on Nick. "What did you do to it?"

"Nothing."

"You're joking."

Phoebe wilted a little but squared her shoulders and fessed up. "I didn't want it to suffer. It was suffering."

"What did you do to it?" Ana's tone was softer now, more interested in finding out what happened.

"I beat it over the head."

This hung in the air for a few seconds of silence. A wet sawing sound came from the countertop where Jay was working on the fish. All of a sudden, it stopped and Jay groaned. From his place seated on the easy chair by the stove, Nick thought he saw little bits of fish guts writhing around, squirming at first, twitching half-heartedly, then finally lying still. Jay turned around guiltily, hoping the conversation would resume. All eyes were turned on him. His face spelled disaster, and he knew it. He put down the knife and washed the blood and fish guts off his hands.

"What's up?" Nick asked, trying to sound optimistic.

"Well, I'm not 100 percent sure."

"But what?" Phoebe asked. An edge had come into her voice.

"Well, you know how I said the fish looked kind of fat?"

"Yes."

"It's a perch. That's what's called a panfish. I knew it shouldn't have been that fat, and I think I even said so."

"Oh, fuck," said Chris, realizing first. Nick hung his head.

"What?" Ana spat at Jay.

"She was pregnant."

The whine of a snowmobile a mile off drifted in through the crack beneath the door. The wind moaned against the windowpanes briefly, then died down.

"How do you know?" Ana finally asked in disbelief.

"Go take a look for yourself."

Everyone stayed where they were for quite a long time. Between the wind on the windowpanes and the occasional snowmobile, there were things to break the silence. All five of them felt that the whole thing was somehow their personal fault.

"I'm hungry," said Chris, finally, which was somehow once again the perfect thing to say.

"I guess," Nick said, "we should get ready for dinner." They filed, defeated, into their rooms, and Jay sat morosely feeding the stove, wondering what he could do to save the weekend.

Fortunately, he thought, we're on to the part of the evening that involves spending money indoors. We should be on solid ground. He went to take a shower and wondered what they would talk about at the bar.

* * *

Morning snuck through the windows like a truant—everyone who was awake before dawn felt that it remained dark for far too long, but then suddenly gray blue light seeped in under the curtains, and it wasn't welcome; it barged in too quickly, without the proper ceremony. The warmth of his weighted blanket, the turning in his stomach, and the pulsing static in his mind kept Jay in bed for half an hour after dawn broke. He tried to remember what they'd talked about at the bar the night before while he pulled on a second pair of socks. Moving slowly, half-expecting someone to be waiting by the dead stove to complain about the heat, Jay left his room and closed the door. The front room was empty, the bed of embers in the stove still orange and flickering weakly. Jay braced himself, pulled on his gloves and hat, and opened the back door.

The first icy blast to the face is an acquired taste, but once you acquired it, the shock is a pleasure like a sauna or an ice bath. It was so blustery that Jay couldn't tell if any snow was actually falling or if the angry winds were merely rushing through the woods blowing snow from the pine boughs like an angry toddler sweeping his arm across a countertop. He walked out toward the woodshed and began to sink thigh-deep in the snow about ten feet from the door, soldiering on after a moment of wondering whether to return for the snowshoes. His lungs heaved and burned by the time he reached the little green shed where the chopping block and splitting maul stayed in the winter. Immediately, he shed a layer, picked up the maul, set a log, and got to work.

A good splitting session, one where the wood was dry and his swings were true and the need wasn't too urgent, did wonders for his mood. Once the pile of stove wood had grown to a few armfuls, Jay swung the maul into the block and loaded up one arm, then the other, wobbling and shifting so as not to drop the overflowing load. Fighting back through the snow, he dropped about a dozen pieces, and he tracked a bunch of snow into the house while dropping the load in the box beside the stove, and when he went back out, he had just enough arm space for the last of the stove pieces, but not the jacket that he'd shed, so he had to set the load down and put the jacket on and load up again. By the time he pulled off his boots and swept up the snow, he was sweaty and frazzled and ready to be angry at the next poor thing he encountered, which was Phoebe, in flannel pajamas and a green beanie and mittens, sitting on the arm of the easy chair watching him fight with his layers as he peeled them off, one sleeve at a time.

"Good morning," he said, kneeling down by the stove, poking the coals, and feeding in pieces from the fresh load.

She sat down in the easy chair, looking first at the stove and then around, eyes finally settling on something to Jay's left. "That wouldn't happen to be a kettle, would it?" Her eyes widened. "Oh, my God. And a French press?"

"Sure is. On both counts."

"Well, what the hell," she said, smiling.

"I'm sorry. I was so hungover yesterday I could barely walk."

"I'm just giving you a hard time. But I am glad I made it for today's batch."

"I don't have milk or anything."

"That's fine. Nick bullied me out of milk and sugar because he says it's too many steps. Some days you run out of sugar or milk but you still want your coffee. I've gotten used to it."

"I taught him that one," said Jay. "That's funny. Most of the coffee he and I drank together was full of sugar and crap. He loved the sweet drinks in high school. Frappuccinos and shit."

The fire was growing quickly now. Jay tossed in three more pieces and closed the door.

He sat on the rocking chair opposite Phoebe in front of the stove. He got up, filled the kettle at the sink, and set it on top of the stove. For an eternal five minutes, they stared at the glowing orange seams in the great old iron stove, the circles around the plates on top and the edges of the oven door.

Jay was upset he hadn't made any conversation when abruptly a door hinge creaked and Nick, in the same pajama bottoms and a Blackhawks hoodie, came padding out.

"Morning, guys," he said, plopping down in the rocking chair next to Jay.

"Phoebe tells me you drink black coffee now?" Jay asked Nick with a smile.

"Dude, I know. Aren't you proud of me?"

"Mostly I'm glad we can share a cup this morning."

Nick's jaw dropped. "Oh, shit! The kettles on! And the French press! You must be the classiest guy in a hundred-mile radius. Incredible, dude, thank you. I need it. I'm a little foggy."

"It'll take a while, but she'll be ready for breakfast." Jay looked back at the fire, trying not to bristle. His French press had been a gift from an ice-fishing buddy. The same buddy did spectacular pour overs most mornings in his own kitchen.

"What are we doing today?" Phoebe asked.

"Anything you guys want," said Jay.

"Well, what should we want?" Nick asked.

"Huh. Well you know me, I'd say let's go outside, but we were outside all day yesterday, and I don't want to step on toes. I've got a bag of mushrooms burning a hole in my sock drawer," he said, hoping to shock them with a rough joke. "We could go up to the brewery in Eagle River, or there's this coffee shop with board games in town, or—

"Mushrooms? Like, as in shrooms?" Phoebe was suddenly serious.

"Indeed," said Jay, nervous already about her enthusiasm.

Phoebe looked at Nick. "Would you be down, or…."

Nick shrugged, smiling. "I'd love to. Might be a microdose for me, but all the same."

Jay looked at them back and forth. "Hold on. Seriously?"

They both nodded vigorously. "Well, shit," said Jay. "Maybe take a dose after breakfast, then go for a snowshoe in the forest? I can stay sober and drive you guys out to the Nicolet National Forest. The trails out there are spectacular."

"That'd be awesome. Yeah, absolutely let's do that," said Phoebe, bouncing up and down with excitement.

In the back of his mind, Jay wondered about shrooms and Ana, but he couldn't bear to bust up the stoke with an inquiry. Nick and Phoebe started jabbering back and forth about different trips of theirs, and how they'd never tripped in the winter, and so on and so forth. Shortly, they heard Chris and Ana descending the stairs, and Jay found the kettle nearly boiling, and all of a sudden the day was in motion, voices and rattling windows and creaky boards and pots and dishware all clinking and knocking to the pulse of the newly born day. Jay thought about how much of his stash he was willing to give to everyone, to blow on this one trip, as he fried up eggs and cheddar cheese and spinach and set bread toasting on the stove.

Over breakfast, Nick gently pitched the idea of tripping and heading out to the national forest for a hike. To his surprise, Chris was enthusiastic, and all Ana said was that she wanted to make it to the hot tub before they went out to the bars.

"Oh, I can't imagine we'll hike longer than a few hours," said Jay, now very invested in the plan. "We can head back, say, like three at latest? That'll put us in the tub around three forty-five if we bring our trunks." Ana nodded, glad for once to appear agreeable.

There followed an interval of rushing around, of gathering hoodies and jackets and scarves and finding wallets and using the bathroom, but that was over soon. They each took a few nibbles of bitter shrooms from Jay's bag, which nearly depleted it. Outside, they loaded the snowshoes into Phoebe's trunk: Jay snuck himself an extra stem and a cap while locking up. Soon enough they were on the road, Jay at the wheel, Phoebe in the passenger seat, the others squished in the back.

It was a forty-minute drive to the section of the forest that Jay frequented for long hikes.

The first ten minutes on the highway passed in silence. Chris and Ana chattered back and forth about some of Ana's work drama for a while; Phoebe occasionally asked Jay about something she saw out the window. After about half an hour, Jay began to feel the pleasantly anxious tightening of the chest and twisting in the stomach that signified psilocybin in the system. The fat lumps of snow that weighed down the spruce and pine branches took on features, and Jay felt as though he were cutting through the world like a hot knife through butter. Thoughts sped up, and heart rate sped up, and the trees rushing past slowed down. Jay reached across Phoebe and into the glove box for a Bach CD he saved for these types of occasions. The car fell silent as the music began.

Jay turned into the forest on a recently plowed access road; suddenly, they were driving through a fairytale of dense snow-covered pine and spruce and birch and aspen. They wound along the road at fifteen miles an hour, carefully steering around lumps and chunks of ice. Far ahead there was a speck of brown and red, but Jay couldn't quite make out what it was. Everyone stared out the window with slack jaws, gulping in the woods with their eyes like a thirsty person drinks water. The Bach ebbed and flowed, washing over them along with the bumpy rumble of the road.

Closer now, Jay could make out a deer, mangled, surely by a truck, lying dead with its hindquarters sticking into the road. It looked like she'd nearly made it across and gotten clipped at the last second. Jay tore his eyes away and steered around it. The car rumbled over a large bump. From the backseat Jay heard a gasp and a cry. He turned to see Ana rubbernecking with wide eyes and a hand over her mouth.

"Oh, stop the car. Please. Please stop, oh. Is he dead? Jay, is he dead?"

Jay had stopped suddenly and was slow to react. "Um, well." He craned his neck to look.

"Yeah, it does look like she's dead."

"She? She?" Ana was close to hysteria. "How can you tell?" she asked him, voice weak and wobbling.

"No antlers."

"That's two," Ana cried. "Two!"

"Two what, sweetie?" Chris asked, reaching out to rub her back.

"Two girls! Two fucking girls, that's what!" And without warning, Ana wrenched the door open and stumbled out into the snow. Everyone watched for a second; then Chris got out to go after her. In the car, Nick and Jay and Phoebe watched as Chris tried to ask Ana what she was doing and Ana, red-faced and snotty with rage and tears ignored him, marching up to a spruce tree and tearing off a long bough and dismembering it.

Eventually, Chris stopped talking and just watched her. She tore little bits off, small sections of bristled branches, and arranged them delicately around the dead doe's head. She closed its eyes gently, then set about covering the bloody, mashed midsection with snow. She kept tossing on handfuls and packing it down until only the doe's head remained poking out of the snow. She went back with more bits of spruce until there was a woven snowflake pattern to the wreath around its head. She got up, examined her handiwork, and went back to the car. Chris followed.

"Let's go," she said, jaw set, eyes red but no longer streaming. Phoebe was lost in a trance out the window, examining the individual snowflakes that came to light on the passenger window. Chris rubbed Ana's back and tried to soothe his own nerves, while Nick stared back at the doe in the snow, the head that looked asleep poking out of a delicate circle of woven spruce, which the bitter wind had already begun to blow away.

                                * * *

Miraculously, they had an absolute ball hiking through the woods on snowshoes. Between the shrooms and the unfamiliar circumstances, the doe incident quickly seemed like ancient history, swept away by moments that rushed along like creek water in the spring. The mood reached its zenith after a snowball fight broke out and everyone ganged up on Chris, who was the best sport of them all and the only one who could handle it without getting his feelings hurt. It was a happy trip. Phoebe kept trying to get everyone to examine the fresh clumps of snowflakes on their jackets, and eventually, Jay teased her about it.

"No, she's right," said Chris. "The air is so shitty in Chicago that by the time the snow gets to ground level, it's all dirty and deformed. The flakes out here are dazzling." Phoebe stuck out her tongue at Jay, who looked at a snowflake and watched it melt into his jacket. Spirits were high as they piled into the car to head back. Jay announced the hot tub as their destination and a great cheer went up. He fishtailed slightly as he got back on the access road, and slowed down until he got to the plowed county road. The trees and snow still possessed their pearly edge, though it was wearing off pleasantly.

The memory of the dead doe dawned on Jay much too late for him to prepare himself.

The backseat was talking and laughing, such that they nearly missed the gory sight. Jay was alerted to it when Phoebe gave a little gasp, poked him in the ribs, and whispered, pointing, "Lookit."

Jay realized he should have seen it coming. Covering the doe with snow and spruce branches was as good as camouflaging it. Over the course of the afternoon, at least one and perhaps multiple trucks had run over the hindquarters that stuck out into the road, mashing guts and limbs and bone and painting the snow dark red with blood. The doe's head was twisted, no, wrenched to the side. Not a speck of Ana's spruce wreath remained. It was so much more gruesome than before that she was sure to notice, and so Jay kept his eyes on the road as he listened to the backseat and heard Ana stop laughing, and then fall silent. The world held its breath, and then she gasped and screamed and clutched at her hair as the others looked on, horrified.

* * *

They ended up skipping the hot tub to go home and drink by the fire. By dinnertime, the conversation had lost its narco-meander, and that night at the bar, Ana and Phoebe had had such a crazy streak of luck on the dartboard that the boys were actually a little salty on the way home.

Back at the cabin, they shared a shot of whiskey from the bottle above Jay's fridge. Once the fire was fed and snapping with heat, they all went off to bed.

Jay was up first the next morning, once again feeding the yellow flames as dark blue dawn grew lighter in the windows when Nick stumbled in. He looked around a little bewildered, finally coming over to the stove in his sock feet and sitting down on the rocker with a shiver. Both boys' eyes were bleary and red-rimmed from the night before.

"Morning," said Jay.

"How you feeling?"

"Like dog shit."

"Me too."

Wind blasted the window behind them and when it died, the fire snapped and popped again.

"You back to work tomorrow?" Nick asked.

Jay nodded. "Let's not talk about work."

"You're right. I mean…hell of a weekend. I owe you a huge one."

"Of course, brotha. I get lonely up here. I'd love to see you guys more often."

"Really?" Nick asked.

"Oh, yeah. If my fishing buddies gotta stay home with their families ever, I'm hosed. Every other weekend I go nearly insane." Jay laughed to try to make light of the confession.

"Are they all older than you, or what? What are the guys in their twenties doing?"

"That's them. Married with kids. The ones who aren't are usually into some kind of trouble, or hard drugs, or are gay, but you never know who is gay 'cause most of 'em are ashamed of it. And all the girls up here still think I'm going to marry someone from Chicago.

"They all think of me as the one from Chicago. How funny is that," said Jay, shaking his head. "Mike and Sarah's wedding was the first time I'd been back in eight years."

"Sure. That is nuts. I wouldn't mind having you back in the city more often."

"I could probably manage a weekend or two in the summer."

"I'd really love that," Nick said. He shook his head, looking out the window, trying to express a thought. "Jay, man, I…I feel like just this weekend I've been shocked, like defibrillated, you know, not literally, but…." His words started to catch in his throat. "Like, all weekend, I haven't looked at my phone because it hasn't worked, no service. And we've been outside for long periods, together, exercising, drinking a little at night…. It's like I've been with myself without a break for three days straight. Each day up here has felt like a week. It's so intense." He shook his head, looking to see if Jay was following.

Jay nodded. "I know what you mean. It takes some getting used to."

"I mean, it's great, you know, I love it…but I can't wait to get back to Chicago and bury myself in Twitter and TV and then go to school and be so hands full with the kids that I barely have time to think. I just get through the day and then climb for an hour or two, which keeps me just happy enough to not freak out, and then go home, eat, stare, scroll in my room, watch TV with Phoebe, and it's like this safe little world that's completely shut off from everything. But it makes me feel horrible whenever I have a weekend like this where I actually get out in the real world and experience something new, and I realize that being inside, alone, staring at a screen for hours on end is probably the most wasteful, spiritually rotten thing you could do."

"I hear you," said Jay. "But plenty of people do that out here, too."

"You don't."

"That's because I lost my mind in Chicago trying to fit in. Doing things for myself keeps me sane, and that's the only reason I keep this woodstove and eat so much goddamned fish and turkey."

"Right, I know. It keeps you fit, and your mind sharp, and you've got some community. Like, shit, I should just come up here too. The old-fashioned way will cure my many man-made ailments."

"Don't say that."

"Why not?" asked Nick, distraught, beginning to spiral.

"Two reasons. The first is that I'm cold all the time, and hungry when I run out of fish, and lonely when my three good friends are busy with their families. My hands are blistered, and three of my toes are frostbitten beyond feeling. My daily exercise is usually shoveling snow. I work at the goddamn lumberyard, Nick. So, reason one, the 'old-fashioned way' is lonely and a little bit miserable."

"But look at it right now," Nick whined. "You're fine, and here I am being miserable."

"Well, you're realizing some of the things I realized about life in the city, but it's not your fault. Everyone is a slave to cheap dopamine nowadays. The only way to win that one is to just not play, which I bet isn't an option for you."

"That's what I'm saying," said Nick, exasperated. "The kids I teach learn to read on iPads these days. They don't have a fucking chance!"

"Right, but they do," said Jay, leveling his gaze straight at his friend. "They do. You're in there every day because I know you want to help them. I'm sure there are a ton of kids out there who would all say you're their favorite teacher."

"Maybe. But—"

"No, dude, I'm serious. And the family thing, like, dude. You help kids every day and come home to an awesome girlfriend who's smart and loves what you love. What?" He saw Nick shaking his head.

"What do you think of Phoebe?"

"She's awesome. Hot and adventurous. I'm jealous, frankly."

"It feels good to hear that. She gets on me about shit, I don't know. It's been a bit tough recently." Nick laughed. "Dude, you know what? I go to the bars once a week, and every time, I see girls I wish I could talk to. My buddies bring home girls; I see shit on Instagram. It seems like everyone's got an expensive-looking girlfriend that they can afford."

"But you don't even want that, right? Those girls wouldn't go ice fishing, or snowshoeing, and they sure as hell wouldn't stay here."

Nick shrugged. "I suppose you're right." He shook his head.

"Look, man. That's just life, you know? I sit up here, wishing I had your girlfriend and your life in Chicago, helping kids, actually making a difference—" Nick tried to interrupt in protest, but Jay continued on. "No, dude, I work at the lumberyard. I'm totally part of the problem, all because I can't handle authority and freak out whenever I'm inside for too long. Those are weaknesses. You're out there in the real world, a world as real as the woods or this cabin, helping kids grow up to be good people. That's real, man. Just as real and way cooler than anything going on here."

Nick smiled sadly. "So all this time I've been down there wishing I had your life, you've been up here wishing you had mine?"

"Sort of. Yeah. Exactly."

A door creaked and the boys both turned to see Phoebe walk to the bathroom.

"So, what do we do with that?"

Jay looked at the bathroom door. After a few seconds, there was a flush. The boys knew they only had moments left before people were awake and it was time to pack up and leave.

"Well, between the two of us," Jay said, "we have everything, right? I've got the cabin; you've got the girlfriend. I've got the woods; you have the kids. Just stay in the real world, you know? It hurts a little, but real life—it's like waking up freezing cold and walking out to the woodshed first thing in the morning. The wind feels like it's going to rip your face off. But then it doesn't.

And then you're inside, and your face is twice as warm as it was when you got out of bed. You know?"

"I think so."

"Like, what if you hadn't gotten out of bed, you know? You'd still be cold. Colder than if you go outside."

"I know." Nick smiled. "So you're saying we can't have it both ways?"

"I sure can't. If I could, I'd be in Chicago."

"Really? You'd move back?"

"If I had a girlfriend, I probably would."

"Wow. I kind of thought you'd be up here for life."

"Hell no. After five years...." Jay shook his head. "Hand me the kettle, will ya?"

* * *

After coffee and breakfast, everyone packed up. Jay gave a very similar round of hugs to the one he'd given three days ago. Ana graciously said she'd love to come back in the summertime. Chris and Nick both implored Jay to come south for a visit to the city. No one was quite ready to leave yet. Jay grew uncomfortable over the extended small talk over the hood of Phoebe's car, but when they finally all got in and slammed the doors and drove away through the spindly winter forest, he felt the awful pressing on his chest return, and he wished they'd stayed longer, and he berated himself for not enjoying the visit more thoroughly, and already, walking back inside, he wondered if his old boss at the bike shop in Glenbrook would hire him back for the summer.

Do They Rake the Leaves in Cemeteries?

It was the Saturday before Christmas and the young man decided to ride the bus because the bus was warm. He got on at Brady St. and looked the driver in the face. He rode the bus quite often and was on a first-name basis with many of the drivers, but he didn't recognize this driver, a straight-faced, heavy-set woman you wouldn't want to cross. He sat down in the first row beyond the handicap seats.

Looking around, his eyes met those of a large man talking into a flip phone. The man held his gaze, stopping mid-sentence, then turned toward the window and continued on the phone. "I'm telling you, believe me My'eisha, I'm telling you as a newly reborn servant to my dear Lord Jesus, I'm telling you, you better listen; I'm telling you I see Him everywhere. And I feel Him within me! But you need to be praising Him! I'mma send you the audiobooks—no, you listen now—no—hold on, now I'm just gonna send you those tapes and all you gotta do—listen, girl! All you gotta do is listen. All right. All right." He hung up, snapping the phone closed. He looked at the young man again. The young man looked away, but his devout companion was already speaking.

"This attitude, man! Gets it from her momma. Told that bitch to drop my name when we split, and you know what? Three years later, she still calling herself Trish Thomas, man, Thomas, that's my fucking name! She just don't listen."

"My wife's still got my name. I didn't ask her to change it, though."

"She should!"

"Whatever, man."

"Now you tellin' me she has a right to my name?"

"My Katie said she just wanted to have the same name as our little boy, is all."

"Yeah, man, Trish say that too. It's some bullshit, man, it all is. They just want they hands all up in our shit. It's no good."

The young man thought of the last time he left, red and blue flashing on the front lawn and the trees and past the house; in the backyard, his wife and son already playing catch with a football.

* * *

The off-duty bus driver was cold because he had arrived at the bus stop early, not having been a passenger in many years. The bus rounded the corner and his pulse quickened in anticipation of the warmth and a chance to rest his tired legs. It was an hour's trip to visit his daughter. He stepped back to avoid the splash of dirty snow as the bus pulled up to the curb.

When he stepped inside his glasses fogged up immediately, before the doors were closed.

He fed change into the machine and turned, for the first time in over a decade, past the door of the on-duty driver's cockpit and into the aisle flanked by seats. He looked up when he reached the end of the handicap section and was surprised to see a person he recognized. The young man was looking up at him, confused. A man dialing a flip phone passed, heading toward the exit.

The off-duty bus driver, now a passenger, chose the first row, sitting across the aisle from the young man. He looked the young man up and down, nodded in greeting.

"This side of the fence today?" said the young man, finally recognizing him; they hadn't stopped looking intently at each other. The young man shifted to face across toward his new seatmate, so that a muscular arm rested on the backs of the seats and another in his lap, back leaned against the side of the bus, legs stretched under the seat. He was on the shorter side, wiry, strong once but not so much anymore; his clothes were full, not at all baggy. He looked like a football player, and in fact he'd

88

played tight end in high school, but after the sixth concussion freshman year in Madison the doctors made him hang up his cleats. He nearly got kicked out of the Marines too, later. He had the cockiness of an athlete but was losing the physique; through heavy winter clothes, the bus driver could still tell that the young man's outer shell was a soft one; whatever his sport, his playing days were long gone. Maybe an injury. For his part, the off-duty bus driver had never been any good at sports, and though he'd been an ace in math and science, he'd drunk away college and his first dozen jobs and most of his relatives' goodwill. And so he became a bus driver.

"Yes, sir," he answered the young man.

"And they don't let you ride for free?"

"Never occurred to ask." The bus driver was the kind of man who would rather lose a limb than get a free ride.

"'S'pose you ever pay your own wages?"

"All goes to the same place. Most of those places are far away."

"That's pacemaker money, man. Wouldn't catch me dead paying the boss to ride the bus I drive."

"You got a bad heart too?" The bus driver was a good listener.

"Yeah, fuckin' blows. They're telling me at the VA, they're saying my shit's beating way off tempo, all over the place; they're saying I needed it, but I wish they hadn't. Imagining that shit inside me, I don't know; it makes me queasy."

"I hear you son, but they know what they're doing. Seen a thousand guys like you. They know what you need to keep ticking."

"Yeah. It's fucking bullshit, though. Nobody told me I'd need that shit at thirty. Fucking bullshit."

"You keep feeling like the other day, just don't show up to the hospital."

"Yeah man, did I windmill around the bus or some shit? I got a fat bruise on my hand, I can't even make a fist. I don't know. Sometimes I just swing around and shit." He gingerly pulled off a glove and showed the bus driver a black-and-blue hand, carpals visible, fingers bent and unnaturally still.

"No," the bus driver said. "After we got you up off the road, you flopped on the handicapped seats and the cops picked you up at the next stop. Didn't say a thing."

"Thank God. When I woke up, they told me I came in all hooting and hollering and they had to wrestle me into bed. Woke up as soon as the cuffs came off, they said. I still don't have a clue, man. I mean a fucking clue."

The bus driver said nothing, and neither did the young man. A pile of highschoolers shrieked their way to the back at the corner of Oakland and Kane. Someone named Dylan broke up with someone named Kelsey and presents were being returned for booze money. Tyler's folks are out of town and leaving him alone to watch the dogs so they're having a Christmas party.

They're all so painfully forgiving, offering to cover each other, "No, Sean, I can't," "Sylvia, relax, my grandparents are about to give me five hundred, they do every Christmas." These young people so willing to blindly love each other. Both men got homesick and each, unbeknownst to the other, began casting around for something to say, anything, something. Thoughts of deer and headlights. Finally, the young man coughed.

"'S'pose if they say I need a robot heart, I should ease back on the drinking, huh."

"Couldn't hurt."

"You drink?"

"I did. Like you. My wife is my sponsor. Twenty years next March."

"Oh. Man. I mean, that's great, man. I don't know, though. You know. If that's for me."

"It's okay, son; I'm not here to preach."

"Oh. Um. Well, I appreciate that."

"'Course."

"I don't even drink that much anymore nowadays."

"That so?"

"Yes, sir."

"Didn't think you were the kinda guy who could ever have only a couple."

"Yeah, man. A four pack and some shooters is all I ever get in one huck. Too broke for anything else."

"You're telling me the other day all you'd drank was a four-pack and some shooters?"

The young man said nothing. They were past the college, past the stretch of Lake Drive, the snow thickening and the bus shedding kids as Shorewood turned into Whitefish Bay and the houses went up a few tax brackets. It was solidly morning now but still overcast. The whine and rattle of the bus made it hard to hear what was spoken. At a stoplight, the bus driver spoke.

"I bet a four pack and shooters ain't put a dent in you since high school."

"Look, man, leave it."

"Sorry. It's just I know. I'm the same."

"Are you?"

"That used to be breakfast."

"You ever been divorced?"

The older man furrowed his brow. He knew he would be getting off soon, then starting the half hour walk to his daughter. "Yeah, long time ago. Got married again, kids."

"She keep your name when you guys split?"

"Never took it in the first place."

"Man, what?"

"Yeah, she didn't want to, and I didn't care."

"You didn't feel…I don't know…disrespected?"

"Why would I feel disrespected?"

"I mean."

"Man you're gonna be lonely if you hold on to stuff like this."

The young man didn't know what to say. The bus was nearly empty now, and their voices filled the space, punctuated by the soothing male voice of the MCTS announcements.

"I just don't want a new fuckin' heart, man." The young man had long since developed a contrarian reflex, or, more accurately, dug his heels in to remain as he was. Friends who'd been drinking with him on Brady Street the other afternoon would, if asked, attest to far more than a four pack and some shooters. Things had been going fine for so long. One time his wife was out at brunch and couldn't watch Trevor, so Trevor came on the young man's Sunday morning grocery shop, which included a stop at Otto's to stock up on liquor for the week. His wife had been surprised but happy when he volunteered to do the shopping years ago because he was loath to help in other ways logistically and domestically. He tried his best, but when he was involved, there always seemed to be too many cooks in the kitchen. She thought he just went to Metro Market, of course. He bribed Trevor with a Snickers Ice Cream bar and made the fatal mistake of highlighting a detail that, had it gone unmentioned, would never have surfaced again.

"Hey, Trev, buddy, could you do me a favor?"

"Sure, Dad."

"Don't mention to Mom we made this second stop." He was navigating their rusted Mazda 626 out of the Otto's parking lot.

"All right."

But there went Pandora from her box, and then Adaline, the now-ex-wife, decided to tear apart the cabinets, and there, buried in the freezer, and again behind the cleaning supplies, and again between the wall and the young man's favorite armchair, were things that made her scream. The point was, he said to her when she confronted him, in tears, that it hadn't been a problem until she found out, so why was it now? And she'd said, "Because this explains a lot of your bullshit," and he said, "What bullshit?"

And then Trevor walked in the room and everyone was uncomfortable, and by the time the young man and his wife sent Trevor to his room and went out to the front porch to properly argue, they'd both lost steam and had tails between their legs. But then the following week the young man had fallen down the stairs and into Trevor at the bottom, and although the boy was unhurt, Adaline freaked out and said it was the last straw and he'd left with the cops.

The bus driver was waiting, still listening attentively. The young man did not feel the instinct to flee.

"It was more than that, yeah. More. Pulls from a bottle. I don't know. That wasn't why, though. It wasn't."

"Okay. I couldn't ever stop once I started. No shame in it."

"I know there isn't."

"I'm sorry."

"Nah. It was just a weird day, you know."

The bus driver knew all about weird days. Years ago, he'd been relieved of duties at a movie theater, where he'd mistakenly thought the darkness hid more than it did. His ex-wife and someone else had been blowing up his phone all afternoon. He was supposed to pick up his daughter Hailey from her mom's house, but he'd been too bummed out losing another job. He was behind on rent and was borrowing to pay the insurance on the Toyota whose check engine light had been on for months.

Hailey's birthday was the previous week, and her mom had gotten her a brand-new iPhone, new number and everything. He woke up on a park bench, not unpleasantly because it was May, but his ex never called him more than twice in a row, and his Blackberry knockoff said fifteen missed calls, most with voicemails. He called her, and when they got off the phone, he immediately went back and listened to the voicemails from the other number that had been trying to reach him, the unsaved one, and then after he was done listening he smashed the phone on the ground and cried all the way to the closest gas station, and then he drank from a bottle of Smirnoff until he woke up at a time when both "late" and "early" are appropriate descriptors. When he remembered why, he cried some more. But he didn't need to tell the young man all this.

"I know. Some days your wires just cross. I hear you, man. No skin off my back. Just let me know if next time you'd rather me hit the gas instead." The young man took this in the affectionate spirit the bus driver clearly intended.

"Yeah, man. I'm good now. I'll figure it out."

"Sure you will."

"What?"

"I mean, I'm sure you will."

"All right. Thanks."

"'Course."

They fell silent. The bus pulled up to the curb for a stop, and the bus driver rose. The doors opened, and before he stepped out into the cold, he turned back and looked at the young man. The young man looked back.

"Have anywhere to go?"

"Not really. Just ridin' for the warmth," the young man said.

"Come for a walk." He turned and left, not looking back. The young man jumped through the closing doors at the last second, forcing his way onto the snowy sidewalk. They set off down a gentle slope. The streets of the northern suburbs were quiet. Both men felt the absence of streetlights. It was barely noon, but clouds, fat and gray with snow, made all times feel like twilight. The young man's shoulders were hunched, for he was not well-scarved like the bus driver. Several blocks came and went. The young man saw a new but well-aged and entirely conscious thought.

"It's so much less than it's made out to be."

"How do you mean?"

"Well. You know. Drinking and hearts. All this. So fragile, but not in the way people think."

"Why are they wrong?"

"People act like it's hard to fuck up this bad."

"They're wrong about that."

"I was just having a bad day, man, just drinking, blue, just figured it was the easiest way out for everyone."

"Except the tired old driver who's gotta run you over. You'd be okay with that on your conscience?"

"No conscience. They'd be scraping me off the corner of Brady and Farwell."

"Son, I've been driving the Green Line for twenty-odd years; I usually roll the stop."

"Why didn't you?"

"Guy on the corner waved me down. Pointed to you laid up on the white line. I couldn't see from the cab, but I had the windows rolled down so I heard him in time."

A pause. "I'm grateful."

"I know. But don't tell me it's not fragile."

He wanted to protest, but paused, "I'm sorry for putting you through that."

The bus driver waved him off. "Weird as it was, I'm doing something that I been avoiding for a long time. A good thing."

"What's that?"

"Going to see my daughter."

"Oh."

"Yeah. Been away for too long."

"Where's she live?"

"Around here. Up north." The bus driver had invited the young man on a whim and immediately started exploring ways of ditching him before they arrived together. Some things needed to be done alone. A man ought not make a business of making his business the business of other men, especially this sorry fellow trodding down and out through the end of his twenties. This was not the company the bus driver wished for his first graveside audience in a decade. He knew what would come, maybe not the scale of it, but this was one of those things after which no one ever knows what to do or say. They weren't far from a bus stop; surely it wouldn't be hard to convince the young man to be on his way. But when the time came to gently suggest something, his tongue was tied.

Unlike the young man, the bus driver wasn't a violent drunk, but afterward, several months after Hailey was buried and his wife was gone, he was in the T-Mobile store, trying to get a new phone because the cracked-up one was nearing its end, but also, he made very clear to the worker with the indulgently high chinstrap beard and pink lettered black polo that he needed the old phone because it had two very important voicemails, very important, he emphasized, and he needed a new phone but not under any circumstances at the expense of these voicemails on this old phone. The employee was at first perplexed, then vexed, then annoyed, then pissed off, then threatened, then confused as the bus driver began weeping and showed himself out before security, who'd already been called, even arrived.

He did wish for a body and a brain to know this moment, to feel this with him. And so, knowing the cemetery was less than a quarter mile away, he said nothing and kept walking. They rounded a corner, and the bus driver was distracted, but the young man grew confused, seeing the gates of the cemetery and no more houses. His eyes grew wide, and then he looked at his shoes. He thought to speak before they entered, before his dirty speech could sully the sacred ground of the dead.

"Want me to fuck off?" asked the young man.

"No, it's okay."

"All right. Just say the word."

They stood at the gate, snow collecting on their hats and shoulders. Long enough to hear their heartbeats in their ears.

"I mean, I know it's doing my heart no good. The drinking. And I miss my little boy."

"I hear you,"

And then the young man said, "I just...can't seem to shake it. I guess that's why."

"Shake what?"

"My hands are plagued, man. All I mean by the wrong kind of fragile is that for some of us, shit's just like this. It's just not as bad when you're thirteen and fumbling a football is the worst that can happen. But then you're nineteen and you're fucking instead of running the ball, and then you're twenty-two, and you're drinking instead of crying. And now...no matter how hard I try to shake it. Seems like fate or some bullshit. I hate that but I'm not lying."

"I know. I know you're not."

"All right." And then, "Well, how'd you do it?"

"Shake the drink?"

"Among other things."

The bus driver thought of the long walk home, the longest walk of his life, the walk from the park bench he slept on, home to his wife, listening over and over to the voicemails his daughter had left him from her new number, the number he didn't recognize and didn't pick up for fear of collection agencies, the number attached to a voice begging him to call, saying she was in trouble, saying she took something and she didn't know what, and yes, she'd been drinking, and her heart was beating too fast, and she couldn't breathe, and "Daddy, Daddy, please, what do I do? What do I—"

"It can't be about you. You need to want a better life."

"I'm not so sure about that."

"That's why I said so."

They reached the gate. The bus driver pulled the latch with a gloved hand and opened the gate. He looked at the young man.

"I'm gonna go talk to my daughter. Sit tight."

He disappeared up the path, and the young man began to shiver quickly. He looked around and didn't see anyone and wished he didn't need to pee. It would be easy to slip up the street into a warm pub for a piss and a beer. No more hand wringing, no more dead kids and lost jobs. Just embracing the flaws, the bad, the chaos. Wed himself to them. Rid himself of this nosy old man. Temptation lurked like vultures, sensing the young man half-wished to be eaten by his vices.

But first he was thirsty, and he reached down, and when his hands sunk into the snow he thought of little Trevor squealing with excitement over the "ball snow," the damp, powdery, packable snow that meant weaponry and sculpture to children. He bit a soft mouthful of snow from his glove and it froze his teeth but melted quickly. He held on. He lost track of time and kept saying that he would check his phone and leave soon to piss and drink; he really needed to piss now, and he was thirsty for some old-fashioned water, he hadn't had breakfast and the snow wasn't doing the trick. He counted in his head. He tried to imagine what the trees would look like if they had leaves. He wondered, if there were not snow on the ground, would it be covered in leaves? Do they rake the leaves in cemeteries?

And then the bus driver appeared again, cheeks wet, eyes red, and he walked past the young man, and the young man turned to follow, and then the bus driver stopped suddenly and wrapped his arms around him and cried into his strong shoulder for a long time. And then they left, to catch the bus back south into the city.

It's 4 A.M. Do You Know Where You Are?

You press your eyelids together and count breaths, refusing to let vision enter the equation. You know that seeing your surroundings will ratify disjointed memories, will magnify their already damning implications. When you finally submit, you see the walls of a mostly unfinished basement from a mattress on the floor. There's a poster for the Growlers on the wall, string lights strung from corner to corner. Ripped jeans and band T-shirts of several shades folded neatly on a shittily assembled Ikea shelf. Someone has worked hard to make this dungeon dignified. You turn over and see this particular someone's mess of pale pink hair splayed out on a pillow, facing away. Petite shoulders and hips rise and fall metronomically under thick covers. You recognize this hair.

You manage to get your clothes on quietly enough to slip out of bed and up the stairs. In the living room, you see a scruffy, lanky guy snoring on the couch. You are quickly out the door and down the steps and onto the sidewalk. Your lungs struggle with the hot air; humidity clings to every inch of exposed skin. On the drive home, you play music and skip through every song Spotify suggests, wondering why they all are suddenly fraught with such anxious associations.

When you get home, you remember how your dad used to say that things move more quickly downhill than up. Throw some bud in the grinder and wonder still how plummets this steep are possible. In algebra class, they'd always emphasized the importance of slope, m. Your sense for depressing metaphors was far less keen when high. Watch rays of sunlight slant into your room and grow steeper as the sun rises.

* * *

Thirteen hours prior, you had momentum. Upward mobility seemed not only possible, but probable; prospects were infinite. Work had finished early, and tomorrow was your first full day off. Fresh off a nap and a shower, you strolled with damp hair through the warm summer night and jogged up the steps of Eddie Theiling's flat. Eddie was a fellow spotlight operator and a good friend of Ces, who was interested and whom you were seriously considering sleeping with. She wasn't the kind of girl you bragged about to the homies. She'd actually been the one who'd introduced you to Eddie on the first day. You'd managed to steer mostly clear since she was on scenic, but she still Snapchatted you regularly. When Eddie sent you an Instagram DM inviting you over to pregame, a piece of you suspected foul play. You put it out of your mind. Internal alarms had been a little haywire recently. You rang the doorbell and were greeted warmly by Eddie and Ces and a red-haired girl who was slightly overdressed and introduced herself as Lucy, also from scenery. A seat was offered, along with a beer. The night was on its way.

Once upon a time, the term "pregame" was firmly in your Serious Business lexicon. It put you in the mind of stretching routines, foam rollers, reflex warm-ups, Ibuprofen. It was a time to reflect, to prepare the body, to visualize domination but avoid comfort at all costs, to be hungry for athletic stress. For much of your childhood, "pregame" rituals encompassed your full attention for the entirety of "game day." Your current definition of pregame could not be more disparate, nor more of a fall from grace. As you tap the tab and crack your Bud Light, you reflect that upon further examination, the dangers of playing on cold muscles notwithstanding, showing up to the Opera Theatre company party sober was far more psychotic and, therefore, the stakes of the phrase hadn't actually been lowered, but raised.

The festivities you were preparing for celebrated opening night for the fourth and final show that would then continue to run, along with three others, for the rest of the summer. All four shows had been mounted, dress-rehearsed, and opened in the last eighteen days. During that time, the prairie summer proper had set in. Any more than half a minute outside and you'd be sweating, heat bludgeoning your eyes; heat you could feel inside your hair and bones and teeth. Hours rehearsing in the dark theater sharpened ultraviolet rays against your skin.

The weather had warmed up socially too. Long days together on the catwalk rails connect you to others in a strange way, something to do with watching the same scenes from the same shows over and over again, cramped and shivering under the brutal AC vent above your spotlights. New faces quickly became familiar, and soon enough, you'd forgotten the time when they'd been unfamiliar. The cruelty of picky designers and temperamental directors was an industrial-strength social adhesive. It hadn't taken long for group texts to form and dinner outings to be proposed, and tonight, you'd chosen Eddie's pregame over three proffered alternatives. When Eddie got on the phone to see if other people he'd invited were en route, your mind's eye attached to each familiar name a corresponding face.

"Yo, Tiff, listen…. I'm not saying right now! We'll be here for another forty-five…. Dude, it's like three more minutes of walking…. The hypotenuse!? Fuck the hypotenuse! Just walk an extra four blocks to us! You've seen the Key and Peele bit, right?" He surveyed the room to amused nods from all but Lucy. "Yeah. Of course you have. Come get *high* on *potenuse* with us…. Okay…. Sweet. See you then." He hung up the phone and came back to his seat around the coffee table.

You liked Eddie a lot. He was full of the catalytic energy that kept parties in motion, that dreamt up adventures and misadventures, and he always had a crack no matter the situation. On headset during the shows, he was the stage management's worst nightmare. Each spotlight operator has two channels, one that connects to the entire rest of the crew and another that's just spotlights. The lead SM hears both, but most keep the spot channel turned down low. It just so happened that for *An American Soldier*, the third of the four operas, the stage manager kept the spot channel at full volume. During the third act, Pvt. Danny Chen gets stoned (the punishment) by his unit and commanding officer, pelted with jagged rocks of painted foam and papier-mâché. As the camo-fatigued ensemble hurled rocks at Danny below you onstage, your headset crackled.

"Jesus Motherfucking Christ. Jay, are you seeing this? Did none of these guys ever play catch with their dads?" You cracked up because, indeed, the lack of athleticism onstage was appalling. Many of them were leading with the wrong foot when they threw and looked more like sissies than deranged killers. You were about to respond with a line about pansy ballet kids when you heard the finer pitch of static that was the stage manager.

"Mr. Theiling, please get off com if it's not show related."

"Cindy, I'm talking about the show. We need to spend more rehearsal time on how to throw a fucking baseball."

"Mr. Theiling, I'm going directly to Steve if you don't stop clogging up the airwaves. Spot communication only. Don't make me say it again." You peered through the dark metal forest of the catwalks and could just make out Eddie laughing, looking your way and putting a finger gun to his head.

He was the kind of guy who got away with things. This kind of talk was forgiven because out of everyone in lighting, he was the smoothest with the spotlights and handiest in the shop. He embodied the "work hard, play hard" attitude that you perennially fell short of. Charisma and independence in spades. You finished your beer and asked him where the fridge was for a second; his smile flashed with a silver tooth. He put a smile on grunge, not without allure. You both returned with fresh beers to the living room, and as was typical, Eddie just launched into a thought.

"Tiff should be here by now. Somebody wanna check snap maps? I don't think I have him added." Lucy brushes his thigh and says, "Sure, baby."

"He was active at his place four hours ago." She hands Eddie the phone. He examines and zooms in and scrolls around, then hands it back to her.

"I'm convinced at least half of Snapchat's *features* are a fucking scam, man." Eddie was looking up at the group now.

"Snap maps is so spotty, and like, the speedometer sucks, and half the time I look for geotags, I can't find most of 'em. Well, that last thing doesn't matter, but if they're gonna have these features, they might as well work, right?"

Ces chimed in. "The speedometer totally works! I've done it in the car."

"Dude, I'm telling you, it doesn't. It's at least fifteen m.p.h. off every time for me. Sometimes fast, sometimes slow. No consistency."

Ces shrugged. "I just wish it weren't blocked on the theatre's Wi-Fi. I only get service on the stage right landing for some reason, which is a hike from the breakroom, but I can only look at Twitter and, like, play Candy Crush for so long."

"Maybe you could play a little less Candy Crush and help me with the Act II changeovers," Lucy sniped. She was half joking. "Those stupid beads fuck me up every time."

She was referring to a curtain of bright red beads hanging in the centerstage opening of the *Traviata* set, which looked, depending on your sense of humor, like a flower in bloom or a menstruating vagina. Each petal was rimmed with lights, and the innermost petals were intricately mechanized so that they could close and open, revealing the red beads in Act I and eventually swallowing the dead Violetta back up at the end of Act III. It had been horrible to install. The curtain beads kept getting caught up in the gears and machinery of the petals, so it got moved, but then it was in the way of the lights that lit the petals, and eventually, a meeting had to be called with the scene designer and lighting designer and head carpenter. They all left unhappy. Allegedly. You remember a conversation you'd overheard outside the green room that afternoon.

You said, "You want to know the worst part about those beads? The scene designer and lighting designer live a block from each other in New York. All this confusion about which drawings were right or wrong during the build would never have happened if they had just walked a block or two and had a ten-minute chat in front of the same computer. But apparently they'd both been too busy for anything but email." You really were pissed about this. Your dad was fond of quoting Thoreau, who said, "Men have become the tools of their tools" a hundred years ago.

Lucy and Ces shook their heads in disgust. Eddie pulled a Juul from his pocket, sucked, took out the pod and flicked it, tried again, then got up and went to his room for a fresh pod. When he returned, Ces asked for a rip.

"What kind?" she asked as he tossed it to her on the couch. "Cucumber," said Eddie. "They were out of mint." She made a face but still ripped hungrily, holding it deep in her lungs before the exhale.

"Cucumber is never as bad as I think it will be," she said. "Mint is just better. Freshens the breath."

You laughed. "A buddy of mine at my job last summer said mint and cucumber pods are replacing toothbrushing and vegetables. Just like texting people 'here' is replacing knockers and doorbells." Lucy looked confused and Ces forced a laugh, but Eddie snorted and said, "Jesus Christ, that's dystopian."

The doorbell rang, and he rose to get it. Tiff appeared in the doorway, slim and boyish, not a wisp of facial hair. Hands were shaken, hugs exchanged, beers gotten, and after a long pull and a refreshed sigh, Tiff said something like, "So, are we gonna smoke, or are we gonna smoke?"

"We're gonna smoke, fella. Lemme get it all set up." Eddie went to his room, and you heard the clink of glass and running water and the *chh-chh* of a grinder. You scooted away from Ces to make room for Tiff, but she scooted next to you, touching her knee to yours and playfully putting her forehead to your shoulder. Tiff gave you an inquisitive look and sat down next to Ces. Mercifully, Eddie returned with a full bong in less than a minute and handed it to Lucy. Ces gave you a subtle nuzzle and went back to the conversation.

"I hope this is better than the last batch," Eddie was saying, "Shit was indistinguishable from the cig tobacco I added for chongs."

There was some confusion. "Chongs?" asked Tiff.

"Yeah, you know, like a spliff from a bong. Tobacco and pot."

"That's called a moke," you said, "I've heard it called chop and chong, but moke is the true term of art."

Eddie, amused and ready to playfully spar, said, "Well why's that? Chong makes a whole lot more sense on the ears." Lucy got up for another drink. Tiff and Ces were dialed in to the exchange, eyes darting back and forth like it was ping-pong.

"This kid I went to camp with growing up, Bud Stevens, he was the first one to give me one of these. It was my first year as a counselor. All the older guys would slink off to the stables after lunch, before afternoon activities started. One day he dragged me along. Anyway, there was this horse named Moke. He was, like, beloved and had been around longer than the rest. So Bud drags me into the barn, and they're all huddled around a bong by the one little open window. Apparently when they smoked just weed, they'd be left alone, but when they added tobacco, Moke the horse would always poke his nose in the window and snort and whinny and shit. And sure enough, there he was, head poked in the window as I took my first hit. The next year was his last, but we kept the name. Moke."

Eddie, who'd made all the right listening expressions and laughed at all the right times, was on board. "Dude, that's sick. Never calling it anything else. Pack me a fuckin' moke."

"I've even got the same tobacco we used. Turkish Royals. Sweet and spicy. Never used anything else in the barn." You packed one up and handed it across to him.

Ces rested a hand on your forearm. "Shouldn't we be heading out soon?" You checked your phone. "Ten minutes," you told her. She took out a bottle of pills and swallowed one, then passed one to Lucy. You must've looked curious because she put her mouth to your ear and whispered, "Hey, it's Lorazepam, want one?" You leaned away and shook your head no. She shrugged, whatever, and you turned back to Eddie and Tiff, who looked like they were getting ready to go.

"We ready to roll?" you asked, packing one last pinch of bud into the bong. Lucy and Ces rose, putting phones in purses and wallets in pockets. No one answered you, but it was obvious this restless bunch had achieved escape velocity. Tanks were full, missions were clear. Pockets were patted, Juuls ripped, doors locked, steps descended, cars piled into, ignition sequence start, 3...2...1... blast off.

* * *

During your first week of college, you'd made friends with an engineering major, and somewhere along the line, he defined for you the word "fulcrum"—the point at which a lever pivots, where things go decidedly from one side to the other. It was quite clear cut when you applied the concept to scales and playground apparati, but now you were somewhere between beers number nine and twelve and rather wished you'd caught sight of the evening's fulcrum and planted your feet, remained on the side of clarity. But you were well beyond that, still conscious but rapidly losing altitude. Locomotion was now a matter of leaning one way or the other as you tumbled forward, in the manner of luge or bobsled, and hoping that you didn't fly off the track.

Colored lights and slurred, earnestly conversing voices felt like physical obstacles. You leaned on a doorframe and tried to remember what you were doing. You felt a pressure in your bladder and remembered: *bathroom*. You careened past the bar and the little dance floor, twenty-five or so dancing to Destiny's Child. You turned down the hall to the men's room. The wall on your left was lit up magenta; the one on your right was yellow. You threw open the bathroom door and caught sight of yourself in the mirror. *Jesus.* You hoped you didn't look as drunk as you looked.

Halfway through a piss, you heard giggles and sniffing in the stall to your left. You briefly considered inviting yourself in, then thought the better of it. Probably principles, singers, ones that wanted no part of a nearly blacked-out spot op. You ran the tap over your hands. After another disconcerting moment in the mirror, the door swung open and out you went.

You started past the dance floor, headed back outside to Eddie and Ces. At the bar you felt a hand on your forearm, a hand that was attached to sharp cheekbones, dark eyes, and a shaved head.

106

The magnificent young mezzo-soprano who was cross-cast as Annio in *La Clemenza di Tito*. Before you said anything, she was telling you she'd see you at work, that Rachel (who played Servillia, her lover onstage, and possibly also off it, too, but no one was certain) and she were calling it a night. She was giving you the conciliatory look that said she knew how much she'd been flirted with, that she appreciated the effort, maybe even had a chuckle, but also that you never stood a chance. This was now obvious, even in the moments before she'd spoken, but hadn't been a fact until now. You tried to ask her if she wanted to have a smoke, but by the time you retrieved your cigs from your pocket, she was gone. Outside, you glanced around and caught a glimpse of Rachel's legs just before they rounded the corner toward the parking lot. You had an overwhelming urge to lie down exactly where you were.

Tiff and two girls from scenery were at the edge of the patio. You approached slowly. Tiff raised a hand when he saw you and stepped aside to make room. The sturdy, pretty ginger girl across from you is finishing a thought.

"—just think we should keep an eye on her. Is all I'm saying." The other girl, taller, bespectacled, with curious green eyes, mumbled something like, "Okay, I guess." Tiff put a hand on your shoulder and said, "Hey, this is Jay, he's on lighting." Expressions of acknowledgment were exchanged and the green-eyed girl turned to her friend but then looked back at you suddenly with a searching look, a look of suspicion.

"Aren't you Samantha Wauldron's boyfriend?"

When you were ten, you went to a pool party thrown by a coworker of your father. You swam under a float on accident and thrashed around, drowning, until you finally found the edge. This felt neurologically identical.

"Uhh. No. Not anymore."

"Oh. Too bad. I think half the Conservatory has a crush on her."

Nice. "Uh, yeah."

"Wait. Are you, like, fucked up about it?" She sounded scandalized.

"Uh…. Nah, I'm good. We didn't even date."

"What?"

This girl was flogging you and pouring salt in the wounds.

"Never mind." To Tiff: "Thoughts on departure?" He put his arm around the redhead and smiled drunkenly, "Asking the wrong guy." You try to smile, but it reads as a grimace. If ever you were to be thrown a bone…. You pounded fists with Tiff and said goodbye to the girls and turned to an open Adirondack chair. You sank back, closing your eyes. The plastic was cool on exposed bits of arm and leg. The chair felt molded to your exact frame. Streetlight and moonlight clashed on the surface of the little pond down the hill. Noises faded. You tried to erase or jettison large portions of the evening but found they only sharpened upon examination, congealing, soon to be branded in your memory. A chunk of time passed in an instant, and you blacked back in walking in the parking lot with Eddie and Lucy and Ces. You were congratulating yourself on at least leaving with the company you arrived with when Eddie took Lucy's hand, gave you a wink, and said, "You kids have fun and be safe!" And suddenly you were at Ces's car, and right before you got in, you thought to yourself, *Okay, I should do just about anything but this.*

Whoever Was Wearing These Jeans

When the table buzzes with the vibrations of a phone call, both my sleep and my fantasy shatter. The glow from the screen throws a veil of white light on the plywood walls, the unfinished wood, and the wall of screened windows now striated with gray moonlight scraping the branches and the wildflowers beyond the porch.

Suddenly my breathing is shallow and I'm up like a shot. I slide my thumb across the screen a second too late. I listen for a second, but the line is dead. Unknown number, area code from back in Chicago. My battery is under 20 percent, and there's no way to charge it out here in the woods.

I turn my phone off and take a big gulp from the square bottle and listen to the night wind until I'm asleep and everything is okay again.

* * *

Saturday slouches in on a slate of dark clouds. I'm flooded with relief as I piss light brown into the pine needles. Facing a sunny day might have killed me. I crawl back into the bottom bunk; the sleepy fantasy is weaker now, though trundling along with the dying momentum of the waning darkness.

I pulled a tick off my cheek last night. It didn't itch; it only creeped me out once I had it in my hand, imagining how it got to my face. It hadn't bitten me, and it wasn't crawling when I found it. Its legs clung to my cheek, not its maw. I flicked it into the darkness outside and immediately felt guilty. It had been... clinging.

* * *

Jay had only been mildly surprised when I showed up last night, greasy-haired, collar crumpled, red-eyed, nearly mute with despair. I hadn't even called, having driven seven hours straight from work in Chicago. He gave me a hug and told me there wasn't any food in the house.

I'd thought my phone wouldn't work all the way out here. That I might be forced out of my own head if given the space. My stomach dropped at dinner when I spotted a guy who looked like me playing *Pokemon Go*.

* * *

"Cut us about fifty at this length."

Jay hands me the fencing pliers and roll of wire. He's planted a vegetable garden on the back corner of his property. The deer and rabbits, he says, will lay waste unless we build a fence. Kneeling inside the rectangle of posts we pounded yesterday, I snip ten-inch lengths of wire. Jay measures and cuts lengths of woven wire fence.

About a dozen lengths in, I'm arhythmic with anxiety that mounts when I pat my pockets and don't feel my phone. I stand up with a wobble. I think about the least damaging way to ditch this job for a minute and return the call I got last night. It was probably someone from back home. I turned my phone off at the time because it made me feel like I needed to scream, but now, this morning, I feel like I need to scream *because* I neglected the call last night and will have to explain myself this morning.

"Hey, what's up?" Jay looks on, concerned.

I realize I've been staring into space.

"I'm good. I'm good. I need to go call someone back, real quick. Is that okay?"

He shrugs. "Sure, man. We got all day."

I don't remember hustling down the hill to the little cabin, but when I get there, I'm out of breath. I panic, thinking the chilly night killed my phone's battery, all the way up until it turns on and the phone begins wailing with notifications. I look away as my thumbprint replaces the messages with icons. My heart skips a beat as I notice the messages app, whose four-digit tag looks more like an odometer. Emails well over 10K. I tap the phone icon and call the unknown number back.

It rings out. "Hey, it's Cade; leave a message." Cade. Huh. Beneath the roaring in my ears a bell rings, but I can't place it. I decide not to leave a message, then immediately lacerate myself for not leaving a message. I call him again, but then don't leave a message a second time because I'm worried about hounding him, but then, once I've hung up a second time, the whole thing happens again—why didn't I just leave a message? I can't call him a third time, and two calls with no message is weird, and the whole situation blasts my body with cortisol to such an alarming degree that I panic again and turn off my phone just before spiking it like a football and mashing it into the ground with my heel.

* * *

"All good?"

"Oh, uh, yeah. Well, no. Didn't get a hold of the guy. But all good. I'm ready to work."

He nods. The fence is laid out and he's finishing up snipping lengths of wire to fasten the fence to the posts. We work in tandem; Jay stretches the fence taut and flush against the earth, and I loop the wire around the top, middle, and bottom of the posts, securing the wire with a pinch and twist of the pliers. I get into a sort of rhythm.

"So, uh," Jay begins.

"Yeah."

"We don't have to get into it, but, uh, you want to get into it?" He says all this with his eyes up off in the swaying spruce trees that surround us. He says it without an ounce of pretension, and, frankly, I'm grateful he's invited an explanation.

"Well," I say, "I'll tell you this story, and try to keep my emotions out of it. After the school year ended and work slowed down, I crashed real bad, you know, the crying jags, the rage, the bleakness, ideation—I was in bed for about two weeks, during which time I accumulated a bunch of nervous and angry texts from people who thought I was ignoring them, which made me not want to look at my phone, and so the pile of texts grew, you

111

know, et cetera, and all that. Eventually Phoebe, who has dealt with way too much of my hysteria for me to be comfortable, gave me her old boss's number. A flower vendor at Home Depot. Real easy, unloading flowers and arranging and watering them. Gets me out of the apartment. But it turned out to have a sort of reverse effect. Working serious hours at a big box store was oppressive as hell. The whole time working I just thought about everyone I wasn't responding to.

"But then I'd go home and not even know where to start and just watch YouTube or scroll or whatever, anything to distract myself. I had a good week where I called a few people back. But then the next week, people called or texted and I didn't call back and the whole cycle started all over again. I started crying really badly one night, and I told Phoebe I was really, like, physically afraid of getting back to people, like, anxiety-wise, and she tried just gently telling me to call one person a day and let them know I was having a hard time, and they would understand because they loved me. And then she got up to do something, like a chore, and suddenly, I was alone and I freaked out. I had to go scream into my pillow. This whole panic episode lasted through to the next day when I had to go arrange flowers at Home Depot."

Beady sweat has cooled on my T-shirt and forehead. I shiver when a breeze kicks up. The mosquitoes are relentless except during a breeze. We've stopped working and are kneeling in the soil. I reach down to scratch an itch on my stomach and feel a bump. I scratch it, thinking it's a scab. The scab clings particularly tightly, and I have to really get in there with my fingernail, and when I finally feel it tear off of my skin and hold up my finger to look, there isn't any blood. It's a tick. The same kind as before. Had not bitten me. Clamped stationary.

"Tick?"

"Yeah," I say, setting him gently down in the grass. He limps away.

"Flick that fucker outta here."

I feign looking back at the ground. "Ah, looks like he's gone." I brush a hand generally over the grass.

* * *

"So, you're at work?"

"Huh?" I ask.

"You were panicking. Still. In your story. At Home Depot, arranging—"

"Oh, yeah, yeah. I'm sorry." I'm back to earth now. "This is actually the thing I'm getting to," I say, smiling a little and even starting to laugh. "Take this with a grain of salt, but I think it's kind of fucking funny." I take a deep breath of absolutely delicious air. "So I have two cousins who both have been in treatment for eating disorders. Anorexia and bulimia. And, you know, I've had my fair share of troubles, especially before I got on meds. But there I was, working at Home Depot, unloading carts of begonias and geraniums, having my very serious fantasy, which usually involves getting hit by a semi at highway speeds or a hail of automatic fire or getting beaten over the head with a baseball bat. Which all produce a sort of twisted relief, the fantasies. And I'm so focused on just getting through the days that I couldn't bear to do anything but pitch into bed. And that in itself, was contributing to the paranoia and mind-splitting stress.

"And all of a sudden right there at work, something occurred to me that had never crossed my mind. I hadn't eaten breakfast that day. I was just getting past the part where there's a pit in your stomach and into the part where you are kind of in a trance, a little weak and spacey but not, per se, hungry. And I'm thinking about my cousins. And I think shit! I've got it! I just won't eat! I'll starve myself, and then people will see how much pain I'm in. How much my lack of a response is not about them, it's about me, and whatever this crash is. If I'm down to a hundred pounds, they'll have to see. They'll understand the scale of things. So, I decide to just not eat, and see how that goes, and see if maybe people will understand and forgive me then.

"A few hours go by, and I go on one of my many long walks through the store to the breakroom in the back where my phone is charging. I was supposed to text my friend back by one for trivia that night, and it was two-thirty, and that was the Sisyphean lump of panic, you know, *du moment*. So I make my way back to the breakroom to get my phone and text my friend, and I turn the corner…and there's an absolute shitload of pizza. Everyone had already eaten by the looks of it; people were just sitting around, looking at their phones. There was so much left. I took one look, and they told me to have some, and I had to take a moment and think about it, you know, commitment to my plan, and then I went ahead and admitted that whatever my ailments, anorexia wasn't one of them, and I was so goddamn hungry, and I ended up eating five slices and spending the rest of my shift shitting my goddamn brains out in the bathroom."

At this point we're both laughing too hard to continue, but that's the end of the story. He slaps me on the shoulder. I can tell that I've told him enough. That the situation of me being here in spite of having not returned any of his calls for the last two months has been made perfectly clear, and that things really are okay.

He stands up. "Let's finish this corner," he says, "and go get a beer." And I smile, and I feel all right. Awash in something akin to relief. But when we finish the corner and I go back to the cabin to check my phone before we head into town, there are three ominous missed calls. One from Phoebe, two from Cade the Unknown Number. Low battery, 10 percent remaining. And down I plunge.

* * *

At the bar, basketball highlights blare from several TVs. Bottles sweat bullets, and I do too, having returned neither Cade nor Phoebe's calls. Jay and I sit at the bar, and I'm relieved we're in T-shirts and blue jeans and boots because even so we look dressed up. Boots and hats and pants of camo all around us are blurred by torn fringe and a layer of dirt.

"You want to stay for a week?" Jay looks forward as he suggests this, and he says it matter-of-factly, like a psychiatrist recommending medication.

"I can't. I can't, man, I got work, and I'm nervous enough being gone from Phoebe like this. And people keep calling, which means they must need things, and it's just all so *aghhhhhhh*—" I finish this thought clutching my head.

He takes a long pull of High Life. "Okay. Bear with me here. I know none of this is rational. But, uh, why don't you just call them back and see what they need before coming to any conclusions?"

I shake my head. "I don't know, man, but it has something to do with wanting to just be safe with myself, wherever I am, and not be needed for anything. There's a certain kind of relief when you can just be all the way into whatever's going on. And not have to deal with whatever's on the other end of the machine."

"Okay, sure," says Jay, demonstrating heroic patience. "But the opposite is happening. You're distracted right now, and have been allegedly since June, *because* you haven't called people back. Don't you think if you just called Phoebe back, you'd be able to loosen up a bit and be here, with me, or at work, or wherever?"

I smile wistfully. "It all makes so much sense when you put it like that," I say, half-sarcastically.

"Call Phoebe back." He's serious all of a sudden.

"Like, right now?"

"When else?"

"Uh." I feel like I'm under a hot light.

"Go outside and give her a call. You'll be back in ten minutes, and I'll be here." His eyes are the color of cold steel, his jaw set firmly. I know it's an order.

My chest tightens.

"Hey, man," I start, "I'm sorr—"

"Stop right there. Go make that call." I understand that if I don't, I'm going to get my ass kicked.

* * *

Out in the dust amid a sea of trucks and ATVs I do call Phoebe, but she doesn't pick up. It rings out. The little battery icon in the corner has barely any red remaining.

I call again, just to be sure, but again there's no answer.

Now I'm headed back inside, pulse sprinting, certain that something is up. When I accidentally open the door with a bang, the whole bar looks over at me. I close it gently and sit down by Jay, fuming, distraught. He looks at me expectantly.

"Nothing. Didn't pick up." He can tell I'm pissed.

115

"You leave a message?"

"No."

"Why not?"

"I don't know. She called me. And now I'm freaking out about it 'cause she didn't answer." I gulped my beer and tore at its soggy label.

Jay shrugged. "I'm sure she'll call you back. Just answer when she does."

I take a deep breath.

"Now go call your boy." He says it more gently this time.

"No, man, what if I tie up the line and Phoebe calls?"

"Then explain to your boy and switch calls. Come on, Nick. Work with me."

I shake my head. He's looking at me. I wither a little.

I feel an itch on my calf. I reach down with a strange sort of certainty and I wonder, but then I pick off the tick, stationary, not yet having bitten, gripping with desperation (but not with teeth or maw) from the skin above the outside lump of ankle bone. I put him on the bar in front of me to crawl.

"The hell?" Jay's terrible resolve is shaken for a moment.

"I keep finding him all over on me. He won't bite me for some reason, but he keeps coming back. He just finds a spot and hangs on." I watch him navigate around my napkin.

"Dude. Kill it then. Just crush it."

I sweep him defensively away from Jay. "He's not biting me. He's just clinging on."

"Okay, Nick, man, I'm sorry. The same tick has not found you multiple times. What are you even saying? There are millions of ticks out there. Kill that tick or I'm going to kill it for you." And he reached over, but I shoved him sideways, and his stool screeched on the floor, and a flame jumped in his eyes that scared me. I tried to sweep my tick off the counter but missed.

The ringing of my phone shatters out through my pocket. I feel electrocuted. It's Phoebe. "Hello?"

"Babyyyy," comes Phoebe's wonderfully happy voice from the other end of the phone. "What's up? How are you?"

"Hey, I'm all right," I say, and I mean it—suddenly, everything bad evaporates and I'm really all right. "Just worked with Jay in the garden this morning. We're having a beer."

"That's lovely! Well, I called because I have a bit of happy news—" she says, but just then I see Jay get a hold of my tick, on the floor, by a table, and pick him (the tick) up malevolently, and suddenly, my throat constricts and I say something in his direction, but then the line goes dead. I can't hear anything. I realize my phone just died. And I didn't even hear the happy news. And she must think I hung up on her. I press frantically on the power button, but it's really dead now. Which I realize too late I should have seen coming a mile away. I got the notifications.

Just as I begin to tear myself apart over Phoebe being angry at me now when she was happy just a few seconds ago, I look up and see Jay, tick in hand, slowly tearing his legs off one by one, and instead of crying, I just scream.

All Fall Down

Lucas Monticello was born in Hancock, Michigan, eight years after his brother David, but it might as well have been thirty, given their way with each other and the world.

Physically, and in some respects spiritually, they were each other's inverse; they were both broad of bone, but David was fat from the beginning and born with the appetite of one who will be fat for life, while Lucas was sturdy and square, not slim but solid, strong, athletic. David's beard grew bushy in middle school; first a stripe of fuzzy reddish-brown sideburn and a whisper of mustache, then some stubble on the chin, then the neck, until each of those islands connected in high school to form the beard that ever after covered his face.

Lucas was not so lucky. At twenty, during his first week of culinary school, he clung desperately to his shadow of a mustache, thinking that it made him look older, making that classic mistake of those unfortunate young men robbed of true facial hair. David had a patient, confident, staunch way about him that people connected in their minds to his beard and bulk; Lucas was shifty, with a sullen manner that made him seem younger and less mature than he really was, with uncut hair that fell into his eyes. But when all the lights were off and the boys were children alone in a tent with their parents, or adolescents in a cabin with their buddies, or young men in the bed of a new woman (or, for David, a man; either would do), the fact remained that they were actually quite similar. Most of all, they both sailed stormy emotional seas made violent by overconsumption; David of food and Lucas of beer.

Besides his weight, David proceeded through school without attracting much attention. He sang in the choir at church and performed in plays and musicals, toggling between tenor and bass, and practiced at home on the keyboard that their mother got him for his tenth birthday. Several times he was sent away during the summers to do something about his weight; each time, he returned home a little skinnier and was back to his normal gargantuan bulk by the end of October. His mother cried when he went off to college downstate; under her own roof, she at least could be sure he ate nutritious meals—what was to prevent him from ballooning even further without her supervision?

In college, mortality slowly crept onto David's screen (homesick one Sunday, he went to church and listened with fresh ears, and heard things that changed how he understood the world), and by graduation, he'd lost almost fifty pounds thanks to long walks around the edges of campus, in the spring which bore a wealth of visual distractions, the budding and flowering in the trees and the pale legs of women, eager for a little color. He moved back home to Hancock after graduation, did his student teaching at Hancock High School, and went to work teaching middle school history in his twenty-third year.

Having steeped himself in Steinbeck and Faulkner, David yearned to raise his own little farm. Not a real farm; a gentleman's farm like their dad had sometimes described; a piece of land up the hill in the woods with a patch cleared for berry bushes and maybe some fruit trees. A place to camp and farm in the summer, snowshoe in the winter, and work the whole year round as a sort of hobby, raising fruit and berries enough, he hoped, to sell at the farmer's market and maybe one day justify some goats. "Hobby" is perhaps too glib a term for what David eventually did—he crumbled earth between his fingers, sweated and bled to put up proper sheds and fences, raised his own fruit with his own hand, dependent on the agricultural and environmental cycles that made Upper Michigan as harsh as it was beautiful; to David, all this was the truest, purest form of prayer.

He spent weeks scouring the internet for listings, driving out in his truck to walk around any that aroused his interest. He decided on a five-acre plot in Atlantic Mine, right across the bridge and up the hill, but he wavered on it for a month or two and had to pay an extra thousand to close the deal. In spite of this, David and the landowner who was selling off these lots got on well during negotiations, the landowner seeing something of himself in David and tenderized because he was months away from death from liver cancer. The old man insisted on writing detailed handwritten letters that David replied to promptly and enthusiastically. When the geezer died two years later, David went to the funeral and thereafter missed the letters.

Around this time, David was diagnosed with Type II diabetes, in spite of the bits of progress he was making with his diet and weight. A death and a diagnosis compounded to send David into a tailspin, from which he recovered with scars: a much shorter temper and a newly ravenous appetite. The funeral was in February, the diagnosis in April. He hovered around two-eighty all that summer, thanks to all the digging in the dirt and tromping around his acres doing farm chores, but by the following January, he was back over three hundred pounds for the first time since college.

Despite his long-standing health issues, David actually wasn't the one their parents worried about. Lucas had been a chronic subject of heated and prolonged parent-teacher conferences, a magnet for skinned knees, moody and temperamental long before he was an adolescent and well afterward, too. He tended toward sports as a child until his failures as a teammate led him to more solitary endeavors, like drinking stolen liquor in the basements of his few friends' houses. He was a general and specific headache for all those around him with the notable exception of his older brother. David was proactively patient with him and, in turn, earned his deference. They played hundreds of hours of foosball on the rickety table in their basement, and never once did their parents have to come down to break up a fight. Their parents figured most of this out by the time Lucas was in middle school and really starting to cause problems and, thereafter, enlisted

David to deal with Lucas when he did things like slash the legs out from under antique furniture with his hockey stick or, years later, return home from a "movie night" with whiskey on his breath and obviously stolen clothes still tagged in his duffel bag.

"Dude," David would say, exasperated.

"What?"

"Can you chill? Like ever?"

Lucas, wasted, pondered the question. "I guess that remains to be seen."

There were a few more instances of shoplifting, but other than that, from his parents' perspective, Lucas mellowed out during the last three years of high school. To their father's chagrin, David was the one who'd shown interest in hunting during his childhood, despite his weight causing more problems each year out in the woods. No one understood why Lucas, fit from sports and fond of the outdoors, refused to accompany the two of them on hunts all growing up. If they'd bothered to ask him, he would have said that he couldn't bear being the one who always said the wrong thing, broke something valuable, screwed up his portion of the labor. He couldn't bear being the lone sour apple in the hunting party, composed of uncles and buddies and roaring fires and plenty of food. For that's how he'd grown to see himself. It wasn't like he wanted to be the one who ended up crying or pissed off—in fact, he spent a great deal of fruitless mental energy on being agreeable—that's just always how things ended up.

The first flicker of hope came the spring of his sophomore year of high school, strangely enough, in a class called Foods and Nutrition. It earned you half a Health credit and was popular among students because of its lack of paper tests and the food to eat at the end of class, ever valuable in a world of atrophied school lunch portions. Lucas only ended up in the class because a few of his buddies bugged him about it. He ended up loving it; the chemistry and geometry of food and kitchens excited him much more than stardom on the soccer field had, back in the day.

His teacher encouraged him; his classmates were always asking for a portion of his Alfredo, or risotto, or shepherd's pie. Around the end of March during turkey season, he spoke to his teacher, who printed out a few recipes and instructed him on sauces. That weekend, when David, now out of college, and their father, nearing retirement, returned home with a truck of turkeys, Lucas asked them for a single turkey and an afternoon undisturbed in the kitchen.

The result had the whole family gazing at a bashful Lucas with new pride brimming in their eyes. The bird fell apart under the knife, each sauce surprising yet subtle, even the smooth but complex mashed potatoes—where the hell had he learned all this? He told them about his class at school, which made his father laugh. "So you're telling me every other kid in the class is whipping up this kind of thing? Give me a break."

And so it went—Lucas got himself a job across the canal at the Downtowner as a line cook and spent all his wages on good knives and a standing mixer and ingredients for his various experiments at home. His parents delighted in this newfound passion, one that seemed to absorb Lucas' destructive tendencies before they could make their way out into the world. So enamored were they with his creations and creative energy that by the time his mother found his flask half full of warm whisky after lunch the day of his college orientation, it was almost too late to do anything about it, or so they felt. When he came home after two months, down a thousand bucks and twenty pounds, neither of which he could afford, they were shocked but not surprised. He asked for a loan so that he could go to culinary school; they granted it, on the condition that it would be the last of its kind.

"We just want the best for you," his mom said to him, as if anyone wants anything else for themselves.

He nearly made it through. During the last semester of the two-year program downstate, he pissed off the wrong people and for various reasons, solid and flimsy, was socially exiled. It had to do with a girl he'd broken up with, and the girl he'd left her for, and the fact that the two were friends with enough of the same people for rumors to get all mixed up, the result being two women who felt they'd been cheated on and no one certain enough of anything to stick up for Lucas. Someone called in a wellness check on him after a week's absence from class and no sightings. The wellness check found him snoring on his puke-stained mattress, an island in a sea of bottles. They took him to the hospital and didn't let him out for a week, by which time his career as a culinary student was certifiably over.

He returned home to Hancock and stayed with David, who was living alone during his fourth year teaching middle school. Lucas got his old job back cooking at the Downtowner. After three months, he added his name to the lease and officially moved in with David, whose berry farm up the hill was bursting with blossoms and leaves, if not yet berries. He kept in touch with one good friend from culinary school, who was now in France studying or working or maybe both.

Things leveled out for a while, meaning his drinking caused problems only for him, and the signs of it were subtle enough that no one thought to say anything about it. And yet every young man seeks to find in motion what he has lost in space, and Lucas, being a young man, was soon nearly vibrating with the urge to be on the move. His life felt painfully stagnant, as though if he didn't get up and do something or go somewhere, he might shrivel up and die for sheer lack of willingness to get out of bed. The thought of his friend in France haunted him as he shoveled snow from the driveway each morning, and he swore he'd be gone from this place before another punishing winter arrived.

* * *

They'd lived together for nearly two years when Lucas made up his mind to talk to David. The whole process was excruciating. In the beginning, they'd seen each other quite a bit. David took great pleasure in showing Lucas the farm and Lucas likewise in cooking his brother sumptuous meals, but as Lucas' hours got more and more absorbed by his job, the intervals between their meetings grew longer and longer.

After a few months, Lucas stopped going to church with David, as they had done for years, because he was too consistently hungover on Sundays and he felt bad throwing up on God's doorstep, or front lawn, or the adjacent sidewalk if he made it that far. Their lives drove them apart. The thing was,

David as a schoolteacher and Lucas as a line cook had inverted work and sleep schedules. Lucas did most of his eating at work and was an inconsistent grocery shopper, which limited traffic in the kitchen. Weeks on end would pass before they laid eyes on each other.

David had a full and busy life between school and the farm and God on Sundays, while Lucas' life, despite six shifts a week cooking at the Downtowner, definitely didn't feel full. He'd grown to despise the commonplace bullshit burgers and fries he cooked twelve hours a day, hated the mounds of muddy snow that flanked the sidewalks most of the year, hated the way in the summer it felt like he was being teased with the kind of weather he used to enjoy but hated now because good weather only upped the resentment he felt walking back into the kitchen at work. These thoughts and feelings were never too far from the surface, but during the darkest portion of their second winter together in the little apartment in Hancock, in an unusually long stretch in January during which Lucas had not seen David since the previous year—literally—things came to a head.

David, though not without problems, never conjured up problems with his mind like Lucas did. He knew that these long stretches apart were because of their conflicting work schedules, and work was not something to be bemoaned but appreciated, and he had his farm and his berry bushes, and Lucas seemed to have a good group of friends, judging by the consistency with which he was out on the weekends. There were plenty of distractions. But to Lucas, for whom work did not satiate but rather irritated the most sensitive nooks and crannies of his young and aggravated mind, these intervals of separation were unbearable.

Unfailingly, by the second or third week he managed to convince himself that David was mad at him, avoiding him. Every footstep of David's in the morning became to him an explosion, every gesture or sign of Lucas' own presence a potentially unwanted thing, a harbinger of the day soon to come when David left in a fit of anger, or disgust, or maybe just mild annoyance. Lucas became certain of these things and took to avoiding David, thinking that's what David wanted.

As January turned to February during the most recent of these intervals, the mere fact that they literally hadn't seen each other since the previous calendar year (New Year's Eve they'd run into each other at a bar) was making Lucas crazy. He was sitting on the couch before work one Thursday, nursing his second beer of the day and wondering what to do about David. His brother was certainly angry or avoiding Lucas this time; there was no question in his mind. That wasn't the pressing issue, though.

The issue was that their lease was up in June, and if Lucas was going to head south before the next winter, as he'd promised himself, he couldn't re-sign it. He wanted to give David proper warning, in case he needed to find a new roommate. If he'd been thinking clearly, he would have remembered that David had happily lived alone before he'd moved in. But he wasn't thinking clearly, and though he shouldn't have needed an excuse to talk to his brother with whom he shared a home, he felt this was the proper excuse. "I'm leaving and we need to talk logistics." He was miserable.

He decided he'd have to be late to work that day in order to waylay David coming home from school. As it turned out, David came home an hour early. The footsteps on the stairs an hour earlier than expected sent adrenaline shooting up Lucas' arms and through his quivering guts. He pitched the last of his beer in the trash and settled himself in what he hoped was a normal and relaxed position on the couch.

"What's up?" he asked with what he hoped was a normal and welcoming smile. "You're back early."

David, breathing heavily after his ascent of the stairs, set down his book bag and surveyed the room. He looked unusually shaggy and ruddy from the cold. "I am. Tracy Langston is covering my last hour of history. And thank goodness she is. The doctor is waiting."

"Doctor?" Lucas shifted nervously on the couch.

"Yes." He waved his hand dismissively. "It's really not a big deal. They ran some tests last month at a checkup and wanted to follow up about my heart."

"Heart?" his little brother said stupidly.

"Yes. They say mine has been working too hard for too long if you can believe it." He turned and walked into the kitchen, the pine boards creaking beneath his every step. In a moment he returned to the living room with a Coke. He smiled at Lucas, who'd stood up and was looking confused, and wrapped his arms around him.

"Luca, Luca, my boy. I've missed you. Don't run off to work just yet, huh?"

"I'm not due in for another hour."

"Excellent. Foos?" The rickety table of their childhood stood crookedly by the bookshelf.

"Sure. In a second."

"All right." David went into the bathroom and pissed for what felt like a full minute. He opened the door and walked back into the living room, noticing as he did Lucas watching him with concern.

"What's on your mind, Luca?"

He shifted on the couch. "Well, I mean, and this isn't even it, and I promise I'm not trying to micromanage. But, uh, maybe a, uh, Diet Coke?"

A righteous smile spread across David's face. "Excuse me?"

Lucas' words spilled out in a jumble. "I wouldn't have said a thing but you just said… you know…heart problems?"

"In fact, I'm doing this in anticipation of being instructed to cut it out. This will not be the one that kills me, Luca. It's better for me than beer."

Lucas wasn't sure if this was a chirp about his own drinking or a legitimate appeal for support. Either way it put him on defense.

"We should go for a drink soon. I've got an idea I want to ask you about."

David looked surprised. "Sure, what's up?"

"It's a long conversation. I gotta run to work in a bit. But, uh, when are you free this next week?"

"Next Friday is a professional development day. I could probably bunk the afternoon portion."

"I have to work that night."

"What time?"

"Five, same as always."

"Well I'll be done by twelve-thirty, so that's enough time, right?"

Lucas looked upset but agreed. "Where do you want to go?"

David shrugged. "You want to go snowshoeing out at the farm? I got a project for spring I think I'll need your help with. We can work slowly and talk out where it's quiet."

"Sure."

"Well, all right!" David finished his Coke and pitched the crumpled can into the trash. The couch seemed to emit a horrible sob. "Hey, hey, bud, come here," he said, turning and rushing over to Lucas, who'd crumpled on the couch and begun to cry. "What's up? Hey, bud, tell me what's up."

"Your hair."

"What about it?"

"It's longer."

"Um. What do you mean?"

"Than last time I…we…I mean, we live together, Dave. And it's been so long your hair looks different."

* * *

An eternity passed before Friday arrived, but then it finally came and Lucas waited for David, tapping his boot-shod foot upon the dusty floorboards. The snowshoes sat next to Lucas on the couch, the heavy leaden gray of winter afternoon shimmering on one of the buckles, he wondering where David was, now nine minutes late. He might have gotten in a crash somewhere. Lucas could see the empty parking lot through their cracked living room window, the white paint flaking on the frame and sill. Outside, the filthy frozen drifts were eight feet high. February was nearly through.

Just as he was about to crack a third beer, David fishtailed into the parking lot and skidded to a stop beneath the window where he sat. Lucas gathered up the snowshoes and dashed out, slamming the door in fresh exuberance. Halfway down the stairs, he remembered his brother's request that he please bring his sunglasses. Lucas retrieved them from his room, averting his eyes from the box of Cosmic Brownies that jutted out from beneath his bedspread. He was locking up the apartment when something occurred to him. He went back into David's room and shook the box. It was full. He stuffed three or four into his pocket and rushed downstairs to the car.

* * *

David's bulk squished forward against the wheel and sideways in either direction, filling the entire driver's seat. Lucas tossed the snowshoes in the backseat and turned to look at him.

"What's up?"

He shook his head. His broad forehead was wrinkled and tense, his brows and cheeks and jaw hidden in a semi-groomed tangle of brown hair tinged with red. His hair, like Lucas', was straight, longer than usual and combed to one side over his ears. His brown eyes were deep and faintly speckled, full of humor and sadness.

"I'm ready to be out in the woods," he said with an air of fatigue, looking Lucas in the eye the whole time he backed up and turned the car around. "I was up to my neck with Sherry Halstrom all morning... it looks like the kid is getting kicked out, and the mom is coming forward with all kinds of crazy accusations.... Anyway," he said with an expansive smile, "like a hurdler, I will not examine that which is behind me. I haven't been out to the farm since I last took out the compost. Speaking of which, how full did it look to you this morning? Before we take off."

Lucas was less religious than David about composting and thus cagey in his reply. "I think we got a while. It wasn't all the way full."

129

"All right." He nodded, his mass of neck barely hidden by his beard and collar. He skidded out of the parking lot, jamming into gear as the car lurched forward and turned on to the main drag.

"Jesus, dude," Lucas exclaimed as he jostled back and forth with the car. "You forgot your seatbelt."

He was checking over the blind spot over his left shoulder and either didn't hear or pretended not to. "Hey," Lucas said again. "Seatbelt."

"Yeah, I heard you, Lucas," he said, turning to look him in the eye and then back around again, not once looking at the road ahead. "I will put it on, but not while I'm driving." Lucas held his tongue as David changed lanes abruptly, and thanked the lucky stars for four-wheel drive. Dirty snow showered the curbside in bits as they turned past the bridge and up the hill, breaking right on the canal road. The canal was well frozen over, devoid of ice fishing huts but crisscrossed in every direction by snowmobile tracks. The ridge rose up on the left side as they passed houses on the right along the banks of the canal. The snow on the road was brown with sand, the little visible pavement white with months of daily saltings. The sky was low and gray, thick with the promise of snow during the afternoon. David drove with one hand on the wheel as he told Lucas about his plans for the afternoon, and for the spring.

"—just too much at this point, which is good, what we wanted, but now, you know, I feel like I kinda have to expand. I mean, I built those first two patches thinking they would mostly fail, or, I guess, I don't know what I thought, but this much success in just a few years is beyond my wildest imaginings. And the fences are too short—I keep seeing bits bent over and bushes with clear signs of browsing. You know, the deer, and whatever else, but mostly deer, I think. So, but, the deal is it's just too much for the two little patches. Or so I think. I don't know, I mean, you'll get a look at 'em. I wonder how much fence'll be above the snow. Can't be much more than a foot or two, all the snow we've had these last two weeks. But, so that's our task for the day—to figure out how much fence we're gonna need to combine both patches into one."

He swerved back into his own lane, finally glancing at the road, as an oncoming log truck steered wide out of the way. Lucas was focusing with equal parts of his brain on his brother's words and the road before them.

"Sounds good," he said. They turned left up the hill onto Coles Creek Road. David took racing lines the whole way up the hill, nearly colliding head on with a pickup coming the opposite way around the second corner. The creek rushed by on their left, the woods thickening around them as the undulating road wound up to the top of the ridge.

David took a to-go cup of sugary brown coffee drink that he'd concealed in the driver door's cupholder and brought it to his lips. Lucas looked at him and raised his eyebrows. For once he was looking straight at the road ahead.

"Taking a break from your break?" Lucas asked with a pinch of acid.

"This is my breakfast. It's only a little more in terms of total calories."

"Come on, Dave. How much sugar is in there?"

"Enough that I have to shit bricks afterward."

"Are you trying to give yourself a heart attack?"

"Here we are on the way to a walk in the woods to burn it off. I've been swimming every day after school. You saw that bag of quinoa in the fridge, right? And the kale?"

"Sure. I hope they get opened."

"The kale already is. I'm sorry that you caught me with this now, and not every morning for the last week drinking a kale smoothie for breakfast. You know that Emily I've mentioned with work? The one everyone's in love with, including me?"

"Yes."

"She's a health nut. I got her on my case. She's been really good. She was the one who got me on the quinoa and kale."

"There is plenty of fruitful ground," said Lucas, exasperated, "ground which I occupy, between kale and Biggby drinks on the health spectrum." David smiled at this. Usually, Lucas was the one making everything binary, and he the one arguing for nuance and gray area.

"You wanna cook me dinner then? If you're the expert?" said he, looking over at Lucas as he came to a stop and skidded left onto Harma Road.

"Sure. I'm off Sunday. How's that?"

"Fine."

"Fine."

"Will there be beer?" he asked with uncharacteristic cruelty.

"Nope," said Lucas, reddening, and instantly regretted it.

"Deal. See you there." They drove the last hundred yards in silence, the snowy fields stretching out beside them up to the edge of the forest a hundred yards from the road. Lucas wished he'd brought beer along. He'd decided not to in a fit of moral clarity, leaving even the stash he kept hidden in his bedroom and could pass off as recently bought. He left it behind in part because he expected to give David trouble about his awful diet and couldn't very well do that while drinking beer. He really did mean to ease up on the drinking; he just didn't know what else he'd do sometimes, especially in the kitchen. And in the woods, and when it's dark, and in the morning when everything was miserable, and....

* * *

David, usually animated by the prospect of a hike through the woods in the snow, had just been dealt the second bad blow of the afternoon. The first was the evident pain in his little brother's voice during their argument about his diet (he should never have admitted about the appointment with the heart specialist); the second was the fact that minutes later, sitting on the bumper with the hatchback open, snow now gently falling and blowing southeast, the landscape a brilliant white dappled by the brows and greens of the forest, his brother's angst was vindicated by the fact that he was too fat to strap on his own snowshoes. He swallowed his pride and turned to Lucas, whose snowshoes were already on and whose gaze rested sightlessly on the shed at the end of the driveway.

"Say, uh, Luca. Could you give me a hand with these straps?"

"Yeah, here, lemme—what's the problem?"

"Can you adjust them for me?"

"They're as loose as they can go, dude. Once your foot's set in, you strap them on and then tighten them down." He looked askance at David because they both knew he knew how snowshoe straps worked.

"No, I uh, meant...can you strap me up? It's just I can't, you know, reach...."

It dawned on Lucas, and despite the youthfulness of his goatee and windswept mop, that he looked suddenly a hundred years old, the blowing snow forcing him to scrunch up his face and cast lines about his eyes and cheekbones, and he bent before his elder brother. "Sure. Here." He swiftly cinched the plastic straps around David's boots and they rose, closing the trunk bed with a slam and trudging up the mounds of frozen snow that flanked their parking spot. Lucas gave David a hand up and almost lost his footing under the weight of them both. They walked side by side through the initial thicket of pine and spruce and chokecherry, each wishing not to be whipped by the branches held aside by the other and then released, with the added bonus of getting to tromp through virgin snow. David paused before they crossed the small field between them and the blueberry patch in question. Trees hemmed in the property on all sides, but for the most part, besides a few stands of hemlock and chokecherry, their path was clear. They breathed the cold air deep into their lungs and listened to the silence of the wind and falling snow.

"All this, you know," he said, gesturing around at the trees and sky and falling snow. "You can't beat it. It excites me so much, Luca. What else could bring such real joy?"

Lucas examined a flake on his jacket sleeve, fascinated by the geometric patterns still visible in the clumped bits of snow. David breathed in the cold air and thought about how lucky he was to be here with his brother, both alive and sober, out in the woods during his favorite season, to see about a project on his berry farm. Could life be any sweeter? He began to walk again, strengthened by his feeling that all was right with the world and that harmony, if only for a moment, had been achieved.

They stopped at the northwest corner of the first berry patch; all they could see of it above the snow was eighteen inches of fence and a little more of posts at regular intervals. The second patch lay some yards downhill from the first. In certain places the snowdrifts were up to the edge of the fence.

After gazing and thinking a while, Lucas about his own relative lightness of heart at being outside, David about the logistics of pulling up two existing fences and constructing one single fence to combine both patches, David spoke up.

"All right, so I'm thinking, today we pace it off, see how much fencing we think we're going to need when the time comes this spring. It'll be at least May I think before we can pull the old posts and drive new ones. I figured you could help me with that, maybe? It's a two-person job, but we can figure that out when the snow melts. Anyway, shall we both pace it and split the difference?"

"Sure."

David then commenced pacing the perimeter of both patches as though they were one. At the far corner, about ten yards downhill from Lucas, he stopped to rest, heaving out clouds of breath that vanished in the wind. Lucas was gazing at the swaying tips of the pine trees to the west, clumps of snow turning to powder upon impact with lower branches, disappearing in bits on the ground or on the arm of a tree, piled feet high. Fortunately for both of them, Lucas didn't see David windmilling his arms as he toppled over rounding the last corner. It took him several attempts to roll over and get up. Lucas was still distracted looking up into the trees. He turned around as David finished the final leg, the crunch of ice beneath the fresh snow announcing his return from the lap.

"I got sixty-eight for the whole thing. Times three for feet. I feel like I screwed up the corners, though. Go for it."

He watched Lucas slowly, deliberately pace out the new patch. He wondered about the kid—were the recent outbursts cause for concern? They certainly made sense. It had to be frustrating as hell having that much talent and still being confined to fry-cookery. He'd certainly been miserable at first, but when they never saw each other, how could you tell? He'd never really said much about what had happened at culinary school, but judging from their fridge back at the apartment, Lucas had mostly stopped his home experiments with fine food.

It was just so hard, conflicting schedules on top of very different stages in life. But how different were they? Lucas drank, he ate. Sunday used to be their day to romp in the woods after church, or go for a swim during summertime, or whatever seized their fancies. David understood. I mean, even teetotalers like to sleep in on Sundays. And it did appear that he hadn't tried to sneak any beers out on this little excursion; as he trudged back up the hill toward David on the final leg, he looked dead sober, and miserable about it. His vacant eyes were glued to his boots.

"Sixty-one, sixty-two, sixty-three," said Lucas, bringing down his shoe with the crunch of finality. He looked up. "So, what? Call it sixty-five?"

David nodded. "I guess." He did the math in his head. "Hot dog! Just under two-hundred feet. Would have been a pain in the ass having to buy all that extra fencing."

Lucas nodded distractedly.

"Well, shit! This is great. Shall we take a lap and then find us a warm place to sit and a bite to eat?"

Lucas nodded absently. "Sure."

* * *

The bells on the door jingled as their boots thundered on the loose boards of Schmidt's Corner, overwarm even after they shed their layers. A few guys in work boots and camo sat along the bar, talking loudly to the bartender or watching TV. David and Lucas hung their coats on chairs and went up to the bar to order.

"A Two-Hearted for me please," said David, who then looked to Lucas, offering to cover him.

"Yeah," said Lucas, "A High Life. And, uh, and a shot of Kessler, please."

David winced but held his peace. He turned to the bartender: "And, uh, could you throw an order of chicken tenders in for me? Yeah, fries are fine. Actually, could I get some slaw, too? Wonderful, thank you." They returned to their table.

135

David launched, rambling about the farm. "I just hope, I mean, we really should start to get some real fruit, you know, not enough to sell to the grocery store or the monks—you know the monks in Eagle Harbor? The Jampot? I drove up there last summer after I got that first handful I was so excited about; remember, I think I sent you a picture?

Anyways, I drove up there and bought some jam and asked the monk who sold it to me, I just said, 'Hey, I grow berries; any chance you guys would buy them off me?' Because I know they don't grow all their own food, you know, that little property by the lake is pretty steep, I mean they have a few gardens, but, you know, I'm hoping to have gallons of berries. And, so but I asked the monk who sold me the jam, and he said, yeah, if I came back next spring or the spring after with bulk berries, they could most likely take them off my hands. Which I think would just be the coolest thing." He paused, suddenly aware of his ramble, though Lucas didn't mind.

The Kessler sat warm in his belly; he'd realized all along that the day had been a good and happy one; he'd just been in too much of a fog to realize. David's farm project was cool, and he was happy to hear about it. He'd listen to his brother read the phone book, such was the buoyancy in his soul.

"That's awesome, dude!" Lucas smiled. "I mean. That's legit! You're legit either way 'cause berries are growing that you planted, but the Jampot! That's a big deal."

David shrugged. "That's the idea. I mean, the first step was actually seeing if I could produce things I could eat, and work in the dirt, and feel the living earth in my hands, and, you know, that's the part that matters. But if people can eat my fruit enough for it to make a nutritional difference? I mean, how much more real can you get?"

"Totally," said Lucas, still smiling. "Totally. One sec." He got up to get himself another High Life.

"I can do the planting myself," David was saying when Lucas returned with his beer. "It's barely a dozen new ones that need to go in the ground. But I am gonna need help with the fencing. You good to come out for a couple of afternoons in May?"

"Sure, yeah," Lucas said. "Sure I am." Suddenly he remembered something and his smile vanished. "Speaking of which, I uh. I been talking to an old buddy from culinary school, he was in France doing all this crazy training for a while, but now he's back, is the point, in Chicago. He told me he might be able to get me a spot on the line at one of the fancy Chicago steakhouses or something. I, uh," (his eyes bored down into his beer throughout), "I'm thinking about maybe moving down there."

David looked surprised but not upset. "Huh! Well, that sounds excellent…. Steakhouses! I bet you'd like that way more than the Downtowner."

"It's not just that…. You know, the winters kinda suck when you can't go skiing or hiking all the time, and I just work my dick off and drink in the same three bars with the same six people all year round, no matter the weather. I gotta get away from that."

David nodded, frowning. "Sure. Well, and don't get pissed at me, but…what's to say that won't happen there, too? Just, you know, like you put it just now."

"I'm not sure. Nothing, maybe. But then at least I'm somewhere new, a little warmer, not the end of the earth. I just feel like there's so much I'm missing for no good reason."

David's chicken fingers, fries, and coleslaw came. An interval of silence passed while Lucas gulped his beer and David wolfed fries and a tender.

"Look, so, and you know I want what you want, right, I mean, you know, Chicago steakhouses frankly sound like a much better place for you than here, by a lot. I guess what I'm saying is you want it to be about going toward something rather than away from something. Running from things never ends well if it's this big a decision. Stability in life and work—you know, it's not sexy, but you've made good money, and we've gotten some time together—I know, it's been scarce lately, but, I mean, just being close, living together—it's not nothing. Don't run from that."

"But you just said," said Lucas, exasperated, "the steakhouses sound better for me than here!"

"I know, Luca, I know, please don't get defensive. All I'm saying is make sure there's some sufficient opportunity. So that you're running to something, not from something. Which it sounds like there could be. An opportunity. Is all I'm saying."

Lucas swigged the last of his beer and nodded. "I've got to call him and tell him I want a job first. He just offered during a phone call when I was ranting about living up here."

David nodded. He'd cleared his plate of tenders and was savoring the last of the mound of fries. Watching him, Lucas remembered something. "Hey, how was the heart appointment last week?"

David swallowed at some length. "It was all right. They've got me on these new blood pressure meds that make me dizzy sometimes. I asked if I could switch or lower the dose and they said no."

"Was something wrong?"

"No. It was just a few tests. The doctor is worried about my weight."

"That makes two of us."

"Don't look at me like that. This is the one meal out a week I get to enjoy. I think I earned it. I had quinoa and vegetables for lunch every day this week. I'll be back in a second." He got up to piss.

Lucas quickly replaced his empty beer with a full one. His gaze came to rest on the mound of fries remaining on David's plate. He remembered the box of cosmic brownies, three of which were in his coat pocket. Suddenly, his hand shot forward and gathered up fully half the fries on the plate and stuffed them in his mouth. He chewed like a maniac and chugged his beer to wash it down. His pulse was racing, adrenaline pumping. He drank more of his beer, idly wondering if he should slow down before work. The bathroom door swung open and David strode back to the table.

"So when would you go?"

"I'm not sure. Hopefully by this summer."

"Have you talked to Mom and Dad?"

"No."

"All right. Go at your own pace, but they might be helpful to consult."

"I'm sure they'll try. I just need to be sure first myself before I really talk to anyone. That's why I talked to you first. I mean I'm pretty sure, but not 100 percent sure."

"I hear you." David had finished his fries, apparently oblivious of the theft, and was now, having finished the coleslaw, shooting the liquid remains in the manner Lucas had shot the whisky minutes before. Lucas had grown accustomed to averting his eyes at certain points during their meals together.

"I mean, I don't know. You know? I think I do, but then I don't. Shit." Lucas shook his head and finished the last of his beer, rising to use the bathroom. His reflection in the mirror vibrated with concerning amplitude. He wobbled a little bit as he sat back down.

"You ready to roll?" asked David.

"Sure. You sure we gotta leave so soon?"

"You work at five, right?"

"Yeah."

"Well it's four-twenty-five, so we best get on down the road."

Once again, for the thousandth time, Lucas was grateful that David had one foot in the real world at all times. It had been said about Lucas that he "didn't have both oars in the water."

* * *

Ten days passed, David and Lucas each faithfully going to work yet with newfound urgency inspired by Lucas' stated intentions. They made a point of running into each other in the afternoon, as David was returning home and Lucas was leaving. February turned to March, and one day in the high forties sent melted snow streaming in the gutters, dramatically reducing the height of the snowdrifts and turning the sidewalk to an ice rink the following day when the temperature dropped and it all froze. All this, despite the soggy ground and slick sidewalks, harkened spring for Lucas, his favorite season, shaking the certainty of his departure. Was he really ready to leave home just as summer came about? One day, he realized that meant he would have to wait until May, to take a week and visit all his favorite summer spots in the woods and by the lake before heading south for good.

David, meanwhile, was more than a little worried about losing his brother. When he first moved back to Hancock after college, the novelty of his new job and newfound disposable income were enough to keep his morale high. In the intervening two years, however, he'd grown used to Lucas, used to living with another body, grateful for the chance to be an older brother when those chances arose. Somehow the idea of a different roommate was even worse than the prospect of living alone.

The first week of March, David heard from a buddy who was back in town and wanted to hang out. This was a buddy who'd hung around Lucas quite a bit back in the day, so David thought of inviting the friend over for dinner. A date was set for Sunday evening, off for the both of them, and each looked forward to a night of fellowship, the likes of which hadn't been plentiful that winter.

"We got a week," said David as he unloaded grocery bags onto the counters Sunday evening in their kitchen. "Then daylight savings and light all evening."

"Finally. Although it feels weird with the snow still here."

"The snow is always still here."

Lucas sat on a stool by their little kitchen table, watching David putter around the kitchen. David had made him promise not to interfere with his "culinary bullshit," to let David try his hand at cooking dinner for their friend. He was baking a turkey in the oven and had been since he got home from school, heading to the grocery store for more quinoa and vegetables.

"Speaking of which," said Lucas, "when is Tim getting here?"

"He told me six-thirty, which could mean any time between now and eight."

"Well, fingers crossed. I don't think I've seen him since I was in middle school."

"Really?" asked David, turning around in surprise. "Huh. I guess not. Shit." He went back to tip-and-tailing green beans.

Ten minutes later, to their surprise, there was a knock at the door. David quizzically looked up from his vegetable-chopping.

Lucas shrugged. They went to the door, opened it, and framed there beaming was David's old buddy Tim DeRoot. He was a skinnier guy with big ears and a slim skull, which made the ears seem even bigger. He wore a hoodie under his black winter coat and jeans and Chucks, cleaned recently. He stepped into David's warm embrace.

"Timmy! Fuck me, how are ya bud?"

"Not too bad, not too bad…. Holy shit, Lucas! When'd you get so tall, geez!"

"What's up, Tim!"

"Come on in; come on. I got the bird in the oven and the rest on the way!"

They all traipsed jubilantly back to the kitchen, David in the lead. "I'm just going to keep cooking," he said, returning to the cutting board, "but you guys stay in here and talk to the back of my head, I'm listening. Tell me stories, both of you."

Tim and Lucas looked at each other. Lucas inclined his head to indicate that Tim should go first. Tim shrugged, smiled.

"I'm just glad to be back home. Even though Door County's only a couple of hours' drive. I don't know. I was really wrapped up in the place, but I'm done now. I'm back to stay."

"What happened?" David asked. "Sounds like something happened. You didn't say much on the phone."

"Not too much," he said, his face darkening. "Well, plenty, matter of fact. You know how I was down there cooking and working on houses. Well, I met this chick two summers ago, started dating, you know; I was really into her. More than she was into me, I guess. What happened was she had this house, a real fixer upper, way out on the peninsula. It was a beautiful place; she got it from a grandparent that left it to her when they died. I kept offering to do some work on it, and finally she said yes, so I just get to work assuming she's good to at least let me keep living there free and stuff, you know, I didn't know if she was gonna pay me, but so anyway around Christmas this year, she dumped me for this rich-ass guy from Chicago, kicked me out of the house, which by that point I'd done thirty-thousand dollars' worth of work on. So, yeah, that's basically it. You guys got beer?"

Lucas grabbed two High Lifes from the fridge. "Shit, man, I'm sorry to hear that." David had paused his chopping, for he felt this was a sufficiently grave admission. "You doing okay, brother?" he asked.

"Oh, yeah." Tim waved his hand and shook his head dismissively. "I'm fine. I was ready to leave anyway. Rich motherfuckers like the one she went off with. I'm glad to be home."

"Well, shit, man, we're glad to have you."

"Yeah, yeah, what have you guys been up to? It's been what, a couple of years? Longer for you, Lucas; I don't know what I was thinking, but you are older than I expected."

Lucas clapped him appreciatively on the back. "Everyone says I look young 'cause I can't grow shit in terms of a beard."

"Yeah. It's always been the same for me. David, bro, are you still teaching school?"

"I am, indeed. Middle school history and English."

"How's that going?"

"Well, I adore the kids, and now Luca's back to keep me company at home. It does get quiet here, you know, socially. But it's fine. Oh, I bought some land, I gotta show you this place. It's my summer project."

"Damn, how much?"

"Just five acres. Up the hill in Atlantic Mine. I'm growing blueberries."

"All right! That's awesome. Damn, and summer's right around the corner! Can we camp there?"

"That's what it's there for, besides the blueberries."

"Hell yeah. That's awesome."

"It is." David turned down the boiling quinoa, turned off the oven, and tossed the vegetables into the frying pan. He cut a thick wedge of butter and dropped it in with them. Lucas winced and returned to the fridge for his third beer.

"So, Lucas, what're you up to these days?"

"Just work, work, more work. I'm a line cook at the DT. We're short staffed if you wanna cook."

"No shit!"

"No shit."

"Well damn, I'm glad you boys are still here. I was calling around, and so many people have moved downstate or whatever."

David coughed pointedly as he tossed another wedge of butter into the sizzling vegetables. Lucas was indignant at what he took as an attempted breach of confidence about his potential departure. "Hey, enough butter, huh? We don't need to eat it all in one go."

"Yes, we do!" replied David with just a little too much gusto to be funny.

Lucas turned back to Tim, who was wondering what just happened. "Yeah, no, everyone's moving. It's nuts, although I kinda understand. You moved."

"True. But here I am, you know? It's like I never left. Door County was fun, though, not gonna lie."

David took the turkey out of the oven and set it on the empty stove top next to the quinoa and the vegetables. He turned off the quinoa and turned down the vegetables, then turned to face the room. "Tell me tales, Tim. I love the kids, but my life has lacked a certain element of sex, drugs, and rock 'n' roll. Pray supply what I have been missing." His eyes glittered with excitement. Meals with old friends were David's second favorite thing in the world, behind working on a summer day in the dirt.

Tim took off his hoodie and scratched his head. "Well, lemme see. It always got crazy in the summer. I worked with an absolute maniac named Chris; apparently, all the dockhands at the job we did together called him 'Crazy Chris,' which was a good nickname, 'cause this dude, I mean, long-ass tangled hair, huge beard, dude was a metalworker alongside his rough carpentry and framing jobs. I met him at this bar, and he said he needed a hand on a job the next week, and this was right about when things were cooling off with Lena, so I was all over it, in terms of the work, you know, so he picks me up the next day in his van and we drive down to this gorgeous waterfront.

"Turns out the job is some remodeling on a shipping container that this kayak rental company bought and wanted to use as storage or office space or something. Keep in mind he told me, he said, 'I don't start work till noon, and I don't work without a beer.' I honestly did most of the work on the job. But the last day, as we're like painting the windows and putting the finishing touches on the awnings, we get kinda hammered and he catches one of the kayak guides getting high and tells him, basically yells in front of everyone, like, customers everywhere, broad daylight, 'Yeah, man, I was gonna bring the last of my pot plants down here as a little present for you guys, but I got drunk last night and traded 'em to a stranger for a quarter stick of dynamite,' and I'm telling you, we all acted natural but were thinking, *What the fuck, seriously?*"

Throughout the story, David had carved the turkey and combined the quinoa and vegetables into a big bowl. Both he and Lucas raised their eyebrows and laughed appreciatively, though the kind of transaction described sounded reasonable, if a shade illicit. Such things were not uncommon in the Northwoods. David carried the food out to the table, and Lucas grabbed himself a fresh beer, pitching his bottle into the garbage in one motion. Tim was a little miffed at their subdued reaction, forgetting that he'd been more sheltered than they as a child. He felt like he had to follow it up, but then they sat down to eat, and for five minutes, no one said a word.

Finally, Lucas, having finished his turkey and now down to the last few bites of grain and vegetables, loudly broke the silence.

"See, that's the shit that makes me want to leave," he said, in the general direction of the table but glancing furtively at David. "Dynamite and kayaking and getting jobs from strangers in bars.... I know you've just come home from all that, Tim, but if I don't mix it up soon, I think I'm going to become like one of those people who mutters to themselves all the time and isn't really sane. I'd join the Army, but they'd make me dry out." He fell silent, mildly embarrassed.

Tim was confused. "They got all those things here, I'm sure," he said. "Kayaking and dynamite and strangers who need help."

"Sure, but even you had to go to Door County to have some adventures. I mean, shit, you nearly got married, you fucking, you know, did something with your life in a new place. All I do is get hammered making chicken tenders all night, six nights a week, winter, summer, in my hometown. All I do. Even if leaving's rough, at least it'll make me love this place like you do, now, Tim. You couldn't've loved it too much if you left in the first place."

Tim looked like a deer in the headlights, unsure of what he'd walked into. David cleared his throat and said, "Yes, leaving does help, but you need to be going toward something. Not just fleeing what's here."

Lucas glared at him but held his tongue. Tim said, "You, uh, thinking of moving, Lucas?"

"I don't know. Maybe."

"You got a destination in mind?"

"Chicago."

"Chicago's sweet. You got a job lined up?"

"Yeah. Maybe. Guy I went to culinary school with said he could hook me up at this steakhouse."

Tim nodded and shrugged. "Sounds like you're set."

"It's just," Lucas began, looking mostly at David to Tim's annoyance, "it's just once I set the whole thing in motion, and told my buddy I was coming in May, and told some people...suddenly everything around here, my life, is just drenched with like, meaning, and I'm realizing the things I like about life up here, things I'm going to miss, but it's just that that's still not enough to dispel the everyday restlessness that makes me antsy and want to leave in the first place. Like nothing will change unless I change it, and I desperately want to because I'm miserable, but the second I make up my mind to change things, something in me clings to whatever routine or thing is causing the problems in the first place, like I'm gonna miss it. It's like breaking up with a shitty girl," he said disgustedly, finishing his beer and rising to get another.

David reached out his hand. "Hey, Luca. Maybe a water?"

"Suck my balls."

Tim raised his eyebrows at David, who shrugged apologetically, as if to say, I know, but what can you do?

* * *

Lucas fell into a stupor and barely touched his beer. David and Tim went back and forth about the whereabouts of old friends, old girlfriends, who was regularly back in town, who'd gotten pregnant, married, gone to jail, died. Tim complimented David on the food, and Lucas, though he was very drunk, was clairvoyant enough to assent, and honestly, too—it was a relief to taste in the quinoa and vegetables the steady hand of a dish made regularly—David had cooked this often recently. The turkey, too, was juicy and tender, cooked thoroughly but not too much.

Lucas tried to keep his eyes open but soon slumped forward on the arm of the couch and was snoring within minutes. Tim was trying to tell David a story of this time he went ice fishing with these guys and they took a ton of shrooms and one guy passed out on the ice and the others wanted to just let him wake up, "He'll be fine," but Tim was freaking out because the guy was face down in the snow outside of the shack, it was ten degrees and the wind was blowing; he didn't want a guy to die on his watch, so he dragged him inside and made a fire, but then they thought that the ice would melt under it and they would all fall through, still being on shrooms, and then…. Tim's voice grew louder and angrier as the story went on, not in relation to the emotional pitch of the tale, but because David kept glancing longer and more concernedly at Lucas, who was obviously blacked out and slumped for the night. It was clear he wasn't listening, only trying to look attentive enough to maintain politeness.

"Yeah, that's wild," he said when Tim broke off. "I'm sorry. The kid's got me real worried."

"It's all good. He's thirsty, huh?"

"He sure is. I'm not sure Chicago is the solution, either."

Tim paused, thinking. "Well, maybe not. But I think it'd be a thousand times sadder if he drank himself to death here than in Chicago. You know what I'm saying?"

David shook his head, mute, with tears about to spill down into his shaggy beard.

* * *

March wore on, nearly all the snow melted, and still Lucas had yet to truly make up his mind.

Since the dinner with Tim, Lucas had come home straight away after work instead of staying to drink, nursing a beer or two in front of the TV or the foosball table instead of eight or ten at the bar. He was grateful for his weekend mornings and newfound time with his brother, frustrated with himself that it had taken this long to get his shit together and see David more often. Each stuffy shift fry cooking at the Downtowner made him desperately want to leave, but each night, he was grateful to come home to David, usually snoring on the couch, the TV turned to a low murmur. He'd told his buddy in Chicago he was coming; the question now was whether or not to go.

A week after their dinner with Tim, David asked Lucas for a favor. "I'm thinking of having people over for my birthday," he said, still watching ESPN with both eyes. "You think you could cook? Tim got a deer this year and he offered to bring over a bunch of venison steaks. You think you could, uh—"

"Oh, hell yeah. My culinary bullshit, you mean?"

"That shit exactly. It's not this Friday, but the one after that. You think you can get off of work?"

"Sure. Probably."

"Excellent."

The Friday evening in question found David and Lucas, the former in a nice blue button down and slacks, the latter in a tank top and apron, each barefoot, puttering around their respective corners of the apartment. The venison steaks were marinating. The TV was off, per David's instructions. He was rather nervous, as one gets before one's birthday guests have arrived; Lucas was just cracking his first beer of the day, animated by the task ahead and the prospect of a party.

147

David finally sat down at the window, looking out onto the ragged streets of April, awash in his own thoughts. Thin snow fell and melted on the street—in a week, the snowshoes would be useless. David loved the winter and was sad to see it go, yet the thoughts of summer on the farm, driving new fence posts with Lucas, maybe a couple of nights of camping before he left...these were enough to lace the clouds of spring with silver. Summers were hard without the kids every day to keep him grounded.

As wonderful as it was out on the farm, it got lonely, and if the apartment was to be empty as well, something was needed to fill in his social life. A wave of sadness came over him at the thought that this birthday party would be his last big social event for the foreseeable future. The light was long in the windows, but it had nearly died now, and still no one was here. As if in response to this thought, there was a knock at the door. David rose and opened it to find Emily Revord, his colleague at school who taught French, framed in the doorway.

She was a Midwestern beauty, clad in Doc Martens and black jeans stretched over the steep sway of her hips and a black turtleneck, and thin, golden-framed glasses that David had long suspected were fake. She was a blond of German ancestry, not like all the Finns in the Copper Country. Her nose was sharp and her blue eyes pierced you until she dazzled you with a smile that began with her eyes and ended almost always with a laugh. David was mortified to find that the guest he was looking forward to most had arrived first.

"Happy birthday!" she said, and wrapped him in a hug. "Joyeux anniversaire!" David had a momentary heart attack until he remembered that he had, in fact, put on deodorant, a little while ago.

"Hey, Emily, thank you so much! Merci! Come on in! I promise there's more on their way, but, uh, they're mostly my friends who are all terribly lax about timing. So, uh..." She walked on ahead, into the conspicuously clean apartment.

"I see, nice, nice," she said, examining the living room. "I always wonder what people's places look like." David nodded, mute with the paralysis of trying to find something cool to say.

"Let me introduce you to my brother. He's cooking for us tonight." She followed him around the corner into the kitchen, where Lucas was chopping potatoes. He looked up and blanched when they came in.

"Lucas, this is my colleague, Emily. She teaches French at school. Emily, Lucas."

"I apologize, I should probably wash my hands," said Lucas, reaching out his clean left hand and gently squeezing her proffered right. He smiled, his cheeks, like his brother's, more crimson than usual. "Good to meet you."

"What's on the menu, Lucas?"

"Venison steak, fried potatoes, and asparagus."

"Oooh, wow! Fancy."

"A farmer's meal," he countered. "David's buddy got the deer."

"You should make it sound like it's really fancy, though, you know? 'Brined and twice-marinated venison, crispy fried spicy potatoes with fresh-picked garden asparagus' you know, like a wedding menu. I went to a wedding last weekend—you guys seen that movie *Caddyshack*? The steak still had marks where the jockey was hitting it!" She laughed at herself and Lucas busted a gut. David hadn't seen the film and didn't get it.

Lucas shook his head, still laughing. "It's funny you say that, Emily. I had a teacher—so I went to culinary school, not sure if Dave mentioned, that's why I'm, like, cooking tonight and everything—anyway, I had this teacher, old Italian man; he was incredible. I was working this terrible job at this Italian place near campus. One day he came in, and he asked to see me, so I took off my apron and left the kitchen and went to talk with him. First thing he said, looking at the menu, he looks up and he goes, 'Jesus Mary and Joseph, Luca, look at this. Look at this! Listen up; I'm going to tell you something, and you need to remember it and go out and tell it to every single other kid you meet in the kitchen, all right? I trust you. Look at me, Luca. You can't eat adjectives.'"

David laughed, having heard the story before, but it took a second for Emily. Then she got it, and, laughing appreciably, looked over at David. "You never told me he went to culinary school."

"Well, you'll find out tonight. He's phenomenal. Come see the living room." They made their way back into the room with the couch and the bookshelves. David went to turn on a lamp, and warm light pushed out the dark blue of evening, and there was another knock. Heavy bootsteps and voices could be heard milling about on the landing. David went to the door and flung it open.

A phalanx of three bodies stood at various stages of peeling off layers of clothing. They all smiled heartily and dapped David up, the third fellow holding on for a lingering, tender hug. They fanned out as David closed the door behind them, their eyes taking things in and eventually resting on Emily. She was bent over the little bookshelf, glancing over the well-worn spines, the torn corners of pages and covers that were found on books that had traveled in backpacks, on planes, books that had been a part of a life. She pulled out a fat hardcover and looked up with rounded eyes of amusement. "Is this your Forster, David?"

His pulse spiked. "Uh, Emily, these are my buddies, Henry, Sam, and Rico. Fellas, this is Emily. We work together at school."

Smiling, she nodded at each in turn and they at her. "David. Are you ashamed of reading Forster?"

"No, on the contrary. Though that is Lucas' copy."

"Huh." She turned away. David let it linger for a moment, then looked back at his three buddies. "Come meet my brother. He's cooking for us. It's going to be incredible. He went to culinary school downstate, you know, so. Legit." They followed him single file into the kitchen, now filled with the steam and smoke of butter and garlic and frying vegetables.

"Luca, Luca, my boys are here."

Lucas dapped up Henry and Sam, shaking hands with Rico, whom he was just now meeting.

"Smells fucking amazing," said Sam, nodding.

"Hell yeah, brother. Venison, potatoes, and asparagus."

"Good stuff."

Lucas turned around with a potato on a fork. "Eat that shit. Tell me if it's done." David noted the aggression in his voice. Lucas got real worked up in the kitchen sometimes, especially if there was company, and almost certainly if there was drink. David watched as he forced the potato on Sam and a bit of asparagus on Henry, who in their nearly twenty years of friendship had never eaten anything green. He accepted the asparagus, knowing Lucas and wisely noting the look in his eye, but held it, not bringing it to his lips.

"Oh my God, dude. That was the best potato I've ever had."

"You bet your ass it is," said Lucas, giving Sam knuckles. He turned to Henry. "Eat that shit. It'll change your life."

He shook his head. "You know I don't eat green shit."

"It won't taste like green shit, though."

He handed the asparagus to Rico, who ate it, and nodded appreciatively. "Best asparagus I've ever had."

"Fuck yeah it is. Wait till you try the venison."

"Yeah, where's that?"

"I'm cooking it last. Gotta have that fresh cooked. It's over there." He gestured across the kitchen to the counter by the sink, where two huge hunks of venison loin were soaking in a hazy reddish substance.

"What's that, uh, marinating in or whatever?" Sam asked.

"A mixture of saltwater and its own blood."

The boys all looked at each other, nodding and smiling. "Sweet." Rico looked at David and jerked his head toward the living room with a shit-eating grin. "She, uh. What's her story?"

David's expression dried up all at once. "Oh, she's got this boyfriend," he lied, shaking his head in faux disappointment. "It sucks."

"Damn."

"You boys need a beer? We got whisky too, and some Coke in the fridge."

Beers were dispensed from the fridge. Lucas turned around in surprise.

"You didn't tell me you got whiskey. What'd you get?"

David unsheathed a handle of Kessler from its brown bag. Lucas reached out for it, but David pulled it away. Lucas' cheeks reddened instantly. The boys all waved off the whiskey, so David passed it to Lucas with chagrin. He could tell his brother was pissed as he poured himself three fingers and dropped in an ice cube.

The posse followed David out of the kitchen and into the living room. Emily was sitting on the couch reading the Forster volume. She looked up as they came in, smiled at David, and patted the seat next to her on the couch. Henry gave David a sharp subtle poke in his flabby back.

"So, are we doing a shot or what?"

"Yeah, let's do it."

Four shots were poured, tapped against the surface of the coffee table, and shot.

"Chaser, anyone?"

"I'm good."

"No, yeah, we're fine."

David zoomed out again in his mind as Emily and his buddies began chatting and really introducing themselves. This was a better result than he could have ever anticipated, though.

Granted, it hung on him to read the signs from Emily and on one of his boys not taking her home. He realized they'd probably want to go out too after dinner was finished. It was so hard to tell with these things. But that Forster comment was definitely flirty, right? He zoomed back in as he realized Henry was telling a story.

"—but, so and then I call the kid I've got out there, you know, in case the tractors get stuck in the mud or something, 'cause we got GPS telling us where the units are going, and it's just straight up not moving, but this time the kid doesn't pick up, which never happens, so we keep calling him, and eventually he picks up and goes, 'Hold on one moment, please; we're talking to the sheriff.' So we don't know what the fuck is going on. Finally, he calls us back and tells us what happened. Apparently a couple of farmers or their wives or something saw these driverless tractors moving about and freaked out 'cause they saw a tractor riding around without a driver, and called the police about it. Apparently the cops thought he was a prankster and almost took him in. The kid showed the cop an email from me on his phone. That's what kept him out of jail."

The listeners chuckled appreciatively. Emily asked, "Driverless tractors, huh. Is that really going to be a thing?"

"If my company has a say in the matter, then yes, they will."

Rico looked at David. "Another shot? I'm getting hungry."

David poured another shot, and down it went. "I'm going to check on Lucas." Emily was asking Henry something, Sam was looking for a place to chime in, and Rico saw that there was no place in the conversation for him. He got up and followed David to the kitchen, where they found Lucas rubbing down the steaks. His glass was empty, a fresh beer on the counter beside him. He had just begun rubbing down the massive loin.

"All good, Luca?"

"Oh yeah." He looked at David with hurt in his eyes and swilled his beer. David cast around for a gesture of apology and goodwill, reluctantly concluding with "You want me to grab the whisky, bud?"

"Please do."

Rico was watching the rubbing process slowly. "What you rubbing on there?"

"Garlic salt with just a little bit of brown sugar."

"Shit, that sounds fire."

"Oh yeah. You're Rico, right? I'm sorry; I'm focused on this and didn't really pay attention to names."

"That's right, I'm Rico."

David came back in with the Kessler and held it in offering over Lucas' glass. Lucas nodded. David poured two fingers and replaced the cap. Lucas looked at him askance; clearly the portion had been skimpy. He drained his beer and pitched it at the trash can across the room, missing. Then he went back to rubbing.

"You all good, Luca? You need anything?"

"Just leave some of that Kessler for me, huh?"

"Oh, we will."

They watched Lucas go back to rubbing the steaks, whistling to himself now, swaying a little. David looked at Rico and shrugged, then left to go back to the living room where the others were sharing stories about Chicago. They looked up when David and Rico came in.

"All good in the kitchen?"

"Oh yeah. Lucas is unbelievable with meat. I remember when he was still in high school, our dad would make him grill his steaks, even though he was ashamed his teenage son could do it better than he could, since he'd been grilling steaks for forty years. It's a gift. He learned all kinds of crazy pastries and stuff at culinary school, but meat was always his favorite thing to cook."

"Well damn, when is it going to be ready? I'm starved!" Sam rubbed his belly.

"He's rubbing them down right now, about to go in the pan. You'll smell it."

Emily and Henry and Sam drifted back into their conversation about Chicago as David looked out the window. It was all the way dark now. The streets were steady but quiet. Rico tapped him on the shoulder.

"All good, bro? You're zoning out."

"Oh, yeah. Just thinking."

"So, uh…you sure we all good in the kitchen?" Rico looked a bit worried.

"Uh, yeah…what do you mean?"

"I guess it's just…we were just in there; I saw your bro rubbing down them steaks with more garlic salt than I've ever seen. You sure he can handle his booze?"

"Look, Rico. I know Lucas is thirsty. That's a separate issue, but you gotta believe me. Even before culinary school, he was amazing at steaks. All of the best meals I've ever had he cooked. I'm telling you, he knows exactly what he's doing."

"All right, I got you. All I'm saying is he seemed a bit looped from the liquor. Kinda wobbling on his feet, you know."

"That tends to happen. But I'm telling you, the meals he cooks would cost hundreds in restaurants. He's special, man, he's got something—some drive, talent, something special. He's got instincts. They're going to be delicious. Blow your mind delicious, I'm telling you."

"All right, all right. You would know I guess."

"No, sure, I hear you. But I'm telling you. He doesn't miss."

"Well, I'm looking forward to it then."

Emily was tapping him on the shoulder. "You go to Chicago pretty often, right?"

"Not in a few years, but I used to, yeah. What's up?"

"Sam mentioned this bar in the city where, like, it's designed around a bunch of pool tables, and shuffleboard, and, like, foosball, and they have a bocce field or whatever it's called along one wall…. We're trying to remember what it's called. You know what I'm talking about?"

"Shit, yes, I actually think so. Is it on the second floor of a hotel or something?"

"Yeah! And the bathrooms are downstairs and down a long hallway."

"Yes, yes, I know exactly where you're saying. Speaking of foosball, we have a table. You guys want to get a quick game before dinner? We've got a table."

Everyone looked at each other. "Yeah, awesome, let's do it." The foosball table was tucked around the corner. As they gathered around it, they realized they were one too many.

"You guys play," said Rico. "I need another beer." He went to the kitchen as the other four lined up at the table.

Emily grabbed David by the arm. "Me and David versus you two?"

"Sure, yeah. Let's do it."

She turned to David playfully. "Can I be offense? I'm bad, but still."

"Of course."

The ball bounced into play. Emily laughed as she whacked at it with her middle rod, eventually losing it to Sam, who took several shots, each skillfully denied by David, who eventually cradled the ball and fired it up the middle, missing the net by an inch. Henry fumbled the ball, he was not an experienced player, and he fought Emily for it before it squibbed through and back down to David. He lined up a drag shot, paused, and rifled the ball into the back of the net. Emily cheered and squeezed his shoulder. Sam fed the ball back into play. Emily whacked randomly but, somehow, almost immediately scored again. She jumped up and down in excitement. They kept on, and the game finished five to two in favor of Emily and David. Rico came back in just as the game was finishing. Emily went off to the bathroom. Rico tapped David and pulled him aside, though Sam and Henry caught this and opened their ears to listen.

Rico looked pained. "Hey, uh," he said. "Your brother is really on one, getting belligerent. I'm fine, dude, I'm fine; I'm just worried, uh…he was still salting the steaks. He just threw them in."

As if on cue, the smell of butter and garlic and venison wafted in from the kitchen.

"Rico," said David, starting to lose his patience and ashamed by his anger because he'd been afraid of just this. He spoke sharply, taking it out on Rico. "He knows what he's doing. Stop freaking out."

Rico put up his hands, as if to say, "I've done what I could, don't blame me." Emily came back from the bathroom. "Do you want to play now?" she asked Rico. He looked confused.

"Foosball," she said. He smiled at her and assented. Henry and Sam watched the pained look on David's face as he turned and went to the kitchen.

Lucas was rocking back and forth on two feet like those billowy figures that snap to and fro in the parking lots of car dealerships. He was singing, slurring the words of a Stan Rogers ballad, something about whales in the harbor. David went first to look in the trash can; there were at least eight cans with his brother's signature crush.

"—haul it awayyyy, haul it awayyy, just two years agoo you could hear the same shout, as the whales swam free in the harborrrrrrr. David, bro, happy muthafuckin birthday, brother!" He opened his arms and David wrapped him up, afraid of what had to be said.

"Luca, hey. You okay, man?"

"I'm incredible. This loin is gonna blow their fuckin' minds."

"Oh, yeah, I know."

"What's up? You need a beer?" He was slurring badly, struggling to keep his balance.

"No, I'm okay, bud."

"What the fuck? Why not? It's your goddamn birthday, and you're not even drinking."

"I had a few shots."

"Yeah, yeah. You wanna do a shot?"

"No shots, Luca. Lemme get you some water." He went to the tap and filled a glass.

"Fuck off with that. I'm fine. Here, try this." He'd lopped off a piece of venison and held it out to David on the end of a knife.

Intrepidly, David set the water down and looked at Lucas. "Luca, bud. Are you sure?"

"What do you mean, are you sure?"

As though it were a bomb, David reached out, took the bit of loin crispy all around from the butter and salt. He looked at the piece of meat, and, with a sinking heart, with his Willy Loman memory of every delicious bite Lucas had ever cooked for him, he put it in his mouth, chewed, swallowed, and washed it down with beer. He forced a smile at Lucas.

"You've done it again, bud! Incredible. I gotta piss." He turned away and rushed away to the bathroom.

The venison was dreadful. This was a punch in the gut for David. He'd watched Lucas drink in the kitchen since high school, and never once had he produced something truly inedible. Almost always they were delicious, and when they weren't delicious, they were certainly bold and balanced—nothing accidental. Never before had he screwed up a meal from being drunk. For that's what had happened—Lucas had mistimed his binge, jumped the gun, come out of the gate too hot, and had rendered himself unable to tell how much salt was too much. There was a veritable crust of salt the taste of which David, now bent over the sink in the bathroom, was trying in vain to wash out.

After a few mouthfuls mixed with a bit of toothpaste, David stood up straight and looked at himself in the mirror, wondering what to do. He couldn't expect his guests to eat what he'd just eaten—maybe if it had just been his buddies, they could have struggled through it, but after the evening of attention from Emily—the shoulder squeezes and the eye contact and the smiles—there wasn't a chance in hell he would risk it. And he couldn't bear the thought of his little brother reckoning with his first complete and utter culinary failure. It would destroy him.

He was drunk and belligerent...and suddenly, David knew what to do.

"Hey, guys," he said boisterously, bursting out of the bathroom. "Food's almost ready. Let's get Lucas in here and do some shots!" He looked hard at Rico and hoped he understood.

Calling into the kitchen, he said, "Hey Lucas. Come do some shots with us."

"What? Shlottts?" Lucas came stumbling around the corner, holding his hand against the wall for support, and seeing people at the foosball table, he lurched over and said, "Who wants to get their shit fucked up in foos?"

"We're doing shots. Luca, come on. I'll grab another glass." David went to the kitchen, and as he did, he heard Lucas bragging about the food to Emily and Sam and Rico. Henry had followed David to the kitchen. "Hey, man, what are you thinking? He's shitfaced?"

David wheeled on him. "We'll be out of here in twenty minutes. Just roll with it. Please. Call it a birthday present." Henry raised his eyebrows and shook his head, but said nothing as they returned to the living room.

"Shots!" cried David, jovially. "Look at this, Luca! Bottle's almost half gone and we haven't even had dinner." He poured out six shots. "To my little brother, the cook!" They all echoed him and shot the whiskey. He immediately began pouring another.

"Another! To me! The birthday boy!" Emily laughed her wonderful laugh as they shot the second shot. People shook their heads from the strength of the shots. Lucas belched. "You all good, buddy?" Sam asked him with a hand on his shoulder.

"I'm fuggin fine," he said, shrugging the hand off. "I'm...I.... Lemme go check on the venison."

He got up slowly, weaving his way across the room, passing through the door with both hands on the frame. David waited for him to disappear around the corner, then quickly glanced around at his party. "Hey, guys, change of plan. Let's hit the Downtowner. Lucas is having a hard time. You guys get ready while I make sure he's settled for the night." They exchanged confused glances as David followed his brother into the kitchen.

Lucas was leaning up against the counter, head on his arms, swaying as he looked around sightlessly. David turned off the burners that were keeping the potatoes and asparagus warm. He tried a piece of asparagus. It was perfect, which triggered a wave of sadness. Just to make sure he gnawed off another bite of the venison. He had to spit it out in the trash and wash out his mouth of salt again. Lucas hadn't moved from his wobbly place at the counter.

"Hey, Luca, hey. 'Nother shot?"

"Uhhh."

"Here."

David eased Lucas to the floor, leaning his back up against the cabinets. His eyes were lolling and mostly closed. David took his brother's hand, placed the bottle in it, and wrapped the fingers gently around the neck. Lucas was tipping over now, mumbling something, and tried to look up at David. He discovered the bottle in his hand, brought it to his lips, drank nothing, set it on the floor, slumped over, and began to snore heavily.

* * *

David arranged Lucas in the recovery position—on his side, arms crossed, one leg over the other.

He placed a towel beneath his head, covered the asparagus and potatoes with paper towel, took one last look at his woebegone little brother, and returned to the living room. With little explanation, he hustled his friends out to the bar where they had dinner and eventually forgot about the promised venison, the drunk brother, the strange, uncomfortable scene from before.

They celebrated David well, played pool and darts. Emily kept up what David thought was flirty banter the whole night. When they all parted ways, David dapped up his boys first, and had a long hug with Emily afterward, and they agreed that they should go out more often. He returned home and carefully arranged little bits of asparagus and mashed potatoes on plates and set them out on the dining room table, as though they had been abandoned after dinner. He picked up the sorry loin and wet it at the sink and rubbed it on the bits of the plate left empty for meat, leaving spots of crumbs of crust and grease that might have been steaks, once.

Lucas was still snoring on the kitchen floor. David put the covered potatoes and asparagus in the fridge with the butter. He wiped up garlic peelings. He drank a glass of water. Finally, he returned to the dining room, and, satisfied that the scene was convincing, he turned out the light, said a few words to the close and holy darkness, and then he slept.

* * *

Oh April, oh weary ragged wretched April, why must you flip our hearts like a penny and let them drop, roll, skitter away into the filthy wet gutter? Why must you roil our spirits one moment and the next cast them down into the cold bitter cell of false hope? Why must you bury our sweetest dreams, only to dig them up again when our backs are turned?

Such was the state of the Monticello household as spring wore on. The day after the birthday dinner, Lucas called off work. He asked David what had happened, and David told him that he had got a little drunk cooking dinner, that's all. They'd enjoyed a lovely meal, really raved about the venison, and headed out after dinner when he'd passed out on the kitchen floor. Lucas was mildly embarrassed, learning this, but then he didn't remember anything after cooking the asparagus, so he was spared the sharp ache of remembering embarrassing details. He saw that David was deeply shaken, however, which didn't quite make sense. He chalked that up to the one bit of interesting news from David—

he had a total crush on Emily, whom Lucas vaguely remembered from the party, and she'd agreed to get drinks with him that night after his buddies had gone home. David mentioned this to Lucas off hand, but then he brought it up again later, and the following Monday afternoon when they crossed paths going and coming in the afternoon, it came up a third time, and Lucas decided to probe. It was hard to say, but something about the curvy, sparkling blond he remembered didn't square with what David was describing.

"So, uh…do you think she was really flirting, you know, or being nice?"

"I mean, she was smiling at me and squeezing my shoulder and stuff like that all night."

"Some people are just like that. You're like that with me."

"But you're my brother, Lucas. I mean, I wouldn't be so worked up if she hadn't kept doing stuff, asking to be my partner in darts and pool, hand on my back, that type stuff. You know?"

"When are you getting a drink?"

"We didn't set a date."

"So you just agreed, like, in general, that you would get a drink."

"Yes, but—"

"Did you suggest it or did she?"

"I mean, I guess I did, but she reacted like she thought it was genuinely a great idea."

"Hmm. Well, ask her for that drink I guess."

It took a while, but finally David did. They agreed to go to the Downtowner after school the following Friday. Lucas would be at work and could peek his head out of the kitchen for a moment while they were there.

Lucas left for work that day with a twist in his heart; he'd spoken with his friend from culinary school and confirmed that he would be arriving in Chicago on the tenth of May, to begin work at Windy City Prime on the sixteenth. He'd told David a few days prior—David had nodded, eyes far away and thoughts elsewhere, saying all right, he'd figure it out. Then he went on and on about Emily.

Well, so I'll need new shoes, thought Lucas as he trudged across the lift bridge, the sun high in the sky still at five o'clock in the evening. The hills and ridges curved away with the canal to the west, the city of Houghton spread out to the east all along the southern bank. The sides of the buildings and the trees were glowing amber in the sun; the canal, free of ice and glittering, washed gently against the piles of the bridge and lapped at the towns on either side.

A man at the bar had told Lucas of his scuba dives down around the canal, about the piles of empty bottles pitched into the canal beside the outhouse the smelter workers had used years ago when the smelter was still smelting, about the spear tips used longer ago for fishing, about the wreckage of boats of all vintages that could be found at the bottom of the waterway. The man told about how he sent up a beautiful spearhead and continued his search, in case there were more, but then when he was finished and had surfaced, his partner pretended like he'd never gotten the spear tip, like he hadn't a clue what the diver was referring to. "I always knew he was a chiseler, that fucker," he'd said.

Lucas' feet carried him across the bridge, around the corner, and in the door at the DT. He clocked in and headed back into the kitchen, tied on his apron, and prayed for a quiet Friday night so he could keep an eye on his brother. There were a bunch of tickets lined up; the other two cooks were furiously at work. He groaned and got going.

Three hours passed in a blur, and finally there was a lull, which found Lucas and the other two cooks out back smoking cigarettes and shooting the shit. His phone chimed. It was David. He had arrived with Emily. Lucas looked at his coworkers: "You boys mind if I go say hey to my brother? He's at the bar." They nodded and waved him off. He walked back through the kitchen to the front, where he found an overdressed David sitting at the bar with Emily. They smiled at him as he approached and sat down.

"Glad you guys made it," said Lucas, wondering why Emily was looking at him with a strange pity. "How was school?"

They looked at each other. David said, "You first."

Emily smiled at him. "It was good! Thank God it's Friday, of course, but the kids were good today. It's hard, though, spring makes them crazy. I'm doing my best to not snap at them. You know, the usual."

David smiled at her a second too long and looked back at Lucas. "It was good, yeah. Spring is rough."

Lucas wasn't sure whether to be amused or concerned at his brother's behavior. He sensed he was intruding. "Well, can I grab you guys anything?"

"No, we're all set; drinks on the way."

"You sure? I can whip something up that's not on the menu," he said, looking at Emily.

"Thank you so much, but I'm good. We had a pizza party today in sixth period and I'm stuffed."

"I'll tell them to comp a drink or two."

"Thank you!"

Lucas bade them goodbye and gratefully took his leave to the kitchen. He sat back down with his coworkers outside in the back.

"All good with your bro?"

Lucas shook his head. "I hope so. He thinks he's on a date with this girl, but—"

"She two-timing him?"

"No, she's just out of his league."

"So is she gonna run up a tab on him or what?"

"No, I don't think so."

"So, what's the deal? Why are you tripping?"

"I...dude, you don't get it. I love my brother, but he's a fat fuck. This girl, I mean, see for yourselves. She's a babe. The blonde with the ass and the wire glasses and the black sport coat sitting at the bar."

"I'll take your word for it," said one, chuckling.

"Maybe later," said the other, with interest.

* * *

Another three hours passed at work and things slowed down so Lucas went home around eleven. Whatever had melted during the day was freezing or frozen now, crunching under his feet, threatening a wipe out if he wasn't careful. The stars were out above the rugged steel architecture of the bridge. At David's place up the hill, the stars blazed in their millions; you could see the cloud of the Milky Way clearly, and numerous constellations, many of which David had learned. Polaris at midnight in the summer hung perfectly in a gap in the boughs of a hemlock tree.

He noticed a light on as he turned into the parking lot of their building, the living room light by the couch, it must be. He hurried up the stairs and found David sitting mute and despondent on the couch. He had a glass of Coke and a big bowl that looked like it had held cereal twenty minutes ago. He still wore the blue button-down and tweed jacket he'd worn on his date; he still wore his work shoes—hadn't even untied the laces. He smiled weakly as Lucas came in. "Hey, bud," he said, scooting over, "not too tired are you?"

Lucas was rather tired, but that wasn't the point. "No, no, it was an easy shift."

"That's good."

Lucas nodded, waiting. David offered nothing, so Lucas launched into an anecdote he'd heard from a coworker. David tried to be amused; before Lucas even got to the end, he interrupted.

"What the hell was I thinking?"

"What do you mean?" asked Lucas, knowing full well what he meant.

"Thinking that Emily was flirting with me."

"So she wasn't?"

He shook his head miserably.

"Um, so, how did, uh, how did it all go down?"

"The worst part about it was I didn't even have to say anything. She just knew what I was thinking, and as we were leaving, she said something ridiculous like, 'You're fun, David, but this is completely platonic; you know that, right? This isn't a date. You're just nice, and I don't have many friends at work, so....' I think 'You're just nice' is the meanest thing anyone has ever said to me." He shook his head.

"Shit. Fuck. I'm sorry, Dave. I mean, she shouldn't have been squeezing your shoulder and all like that."

"But why not, right? Is it a crime to be friendly?"

"Physically friendly?"

"That's just how some people are."

"All right, sure," said Lucas, an edge creeping into his tone. "But if you look like Emily, you don't get to be physically friendly."

David shook his head again. "That's not even why I'm upset."

"Huh? So what's the deal?"

Tears filled David's eyes and spilled down into his tangled beard, their tracks glistening against his hair and cheek. "Well, so after my birthday party, I started feeling so much better. You know, which is normal when you have a crush. It gives shape to your day, something to think about, look forward to, all that. And that was great, but it was also bigger than that. It became about something bigger than Emily. I could suddenly picture myself with a group of decent-looking friends, going on vacations and to concerts and celebrating each other's birthdays with people other than your childhood friends who are still in town. I could picture myself a little bit lighter, skiing or in a bathing suit. It was like I saw her as a ticket into a kind of social connection. She's always telling me about her trips to Marquette and Milwaukee and Detroit, and all these people and other things." He stopped, choked, coughed, and looked up at Lucas.

"I hear you, I hear you," said Lucas, holding his brother's gaze.

"I'm sorry, Luca. I want you to chase your dreams and go to Chicago and leave me in the dust because that's what you should do. You're so talented, and you've got drive, and intensity, and I know how much you need to have adventures. So go have them. Please. I just—"

"I will, buddy; I will. I'm going to go."

"Really?"

"Yeah."

"Like you told them you're coming?"

"Yes."

"I just—"

"What's up, Dave?"

"I just also wish you wouldn't," David cried, heaving all his sorrow out in a wave. He hung his head on his breast and sobbed as Lucas wrapped his arms around him and rocked him.

After half a minute, the wracking subsided, and Lucas spoke.

"Dave, I—I promise I don't feel good about it either. Sometimes...." Lucas' lip wobbled now, always set off by his brother's outbursts. "You know, sometimes it just feels like I'm just going to be dying somewhere else, that's all. But I—I'm dying right now, Dave. I'm suffocating here, and I love it too, and I'm going to miss it like hell, but if I don't get out and go somewhere else for a while, I'm going to piss my short life away here, and I don't think there's anything worse than picturing that every day on my way to work. All I see are miseries, failures, steaks with too much goddamn salt," and now Lucas broke down and wailed. They held each other close, pulling on each other's shoulders, and then again when the wave of tears had passed.

"There's just sometimes," said David, "when I can't even picture anything ever going well again. Things collapsing—first Mom and Dad, or maybe one of us. I'll have a heart attack soon if I'm not careful. You'll find a way with booze. Or maybe we won't die, but we'll be forced to live as vegetables for being such wasteful, gluttonous pieces of shit. I can picture it so easily. Everything, all falling down. All fall down." He paused, then looked up at Lucas. "You'll call me, right?"

"What the fuck? Of course I will. And visit." The mood was lifting.

"No, I'm visiting you in the city. You need to get you a big city life and then invite me out to live it with you."

"You know I will. I'll keep you posted every week. Hey, uh, Dave? You're gonna be okay, right?"

"Oh, I'll be fine. I'll be just fine." David forced a smile upon his wet cheeks.

"All right. Don't forget. And I'm not leaving until we get that new fence up at the farm."

David smiled. "The ground'll be soft enough for the posts soon. We should be able to get on that in a few weeks."

They talked a little more about the farm, and the spring, and about all the adventures they would have in Chicago when David would come to visit. After a while they just sat on the couch together, and then one fell asleep, and then the other, and the following morning when they both woke up on the couch, each grinned at the other, sure for a moment that things weren't so bad, after all.

* * *

At last it was May. The streets ran with the last of the snowbanks, and the earth grew soupy with mud. It got up over sixty for a few days and, thereafter, the switch to shorts and bare legs, preemptive or not, was made. It was around the time Lucas and David usually tried to camp, though it was too early for camping, and froze their asses off under layers of blankets during nights still in the thirties. The days stretched long into the evenings, boats began to appear in the canal; what blossoms could be seen and smelled were cherished as signs that the great test of winter, for the moment, had been passed.

A week before Lucas was set to leave on a bus to Milwaukee, and then another to Chicago, he and David went out to the farm and took down the old fence. It was a Sunday.

Lucas was groggy from the previous evening; David was fresh and a little manic, having spent Saturday anxiously all by himself. He was acutely conscious that their days as roommates were countable on two hands. The sun blazed, heating the car, so they rolled the windows down for the first time of the season. David drove more slowly than usual, easing in with the brakes and taking turns gently.

Hoppers leapt up in surprise as they got out and slammed the doors. The sky was a bright, pale blue above the tops of the trees; at the top of a hill, the wind whipped around them and bent the grass down in one direction, then another. David unlocked the shed and grabbed two pairs of fencing pliers and gestured to Lucas to give him a hand with a heavy roll of fencing.

"Shouldn't we leave this up here?" asked Lucas.

"We'll need it eventually."

"Won't it take a while to pull up the existing fence?"

"Yeah, I suppose. We can leave it."

They walked through the grass, noticing little patches of snow nestled in the shade beneath certain trees. The smell of pine and dirt and grass filled their noses and made their hearts light with pleasure. Pushing through the thicket that divided the grass from the cleared blueberry beds, they noticed the fence bent in places, either by deer or moose or heavy snow, and they noticed the leaves on the berry bushes were shiny and their edges sharp, healthy. Each pulled on his gloves and steadily set to work, snipping the wire that held the fence to the posts first at ground level, then halfway up, then at the top. They started at opposite sides of the lower patch and worked their way around to each other, sweat sprouting on their foreheads, cheeks flushed, hands wearing down into calluses or the sharp ends of wire breaking the skin slightly, leaving them to wipe the blood off on their dirty jeans. Soon, the lower patch was fenceless; they set to pulling out each of its posts. Some stuck in the muddy ground, but some just needed to be worked back and forth and eased out. Presently, the first patch was all the way done, and they began snipping the wire binding the upper fence.

When the upper fence was fully dismantled, they took a break and drank some water back at the shed. Neither wanted very much to continue working—putting up one fence would be more work than taking two down.

"We finishing the fence today?" asked Lucas, noticing that the sun had sunk significantly in the sky since he'd last looked. The haze of afternoon was upon them—the wind had died down, and for long intervals all you could hear was the rustling of the pine boughs in the gentle breeze, and the whine of some unknown insect.

"I was just thinking about that," said David. "I'm a little gassed."

"You got school tomorrow?"

"Half day. Professional development.... I might be able to make it here at the tail end of the afternoon."

"Well, all right. I'm off tomorrow to pack, but I can come out in the morning and drive the posts if you just show me where and leave the driver out."

David thought for a moment. "How are you going to get out here?"

"Can you drop me off on your way to school?"

David started to say something about how they were in opposite directions of the apartment but stopped himself. "Yeah, sure. That sounds good."

"Awesome. So are we going to Schmidt's now, or what?"

"Don't you have to pack?"

"I'm mostly done. Got all my clothes in bags, books in boxes. I need to take some shit to cook with, but besides that, I'm all set to roll out on Friday."

"Friday?" asked David in surprise. "I thought it was next week."

"No, it's this Friday."

"Well, in that case, we're definitely going to Schmidt's."

The wind kicked up and they paused, listening to its tune as it scraped against the tops of the trees.

"You good to go?" David asked, deep in his own thoughts.

"Yeah, let's roll."

"No, uh. I mean...are you good to, like, leave? You think it'll be okay?"

Lucas smiled and said jokingly, "Hell if I know. Either it will, and you'll come visit and we'll party and it'll be fine, or it won't and I'll come running back like I already did once before. So hey, either way, it's looking good for you, huh?"

"I suppose it does, Luca. Let's go get some food, huh?"

"Let's. I'm thirsty."

* * *

Hours later, David and a guy in overalls carried Lucas out of Schmidt's Corner and back to the truck. He passed out instantly, head lolling as he slumped against the passenger door. David thanked the man who'd helped him haul his brother out of the bar.

"Don't mention it, brother. We all got friends like that."

"Well, I appreciate it."

"Don't let him go too far, huh? Us, we're the responsible ones. We gotta make sure they get home every night."

"Sure. But what about us?"

"We just gotta fit our kicks in where we can, you know? Take care."

David waved, then started the truck and took a good long look at his brother, slumped against the dashboard now. The clock read eight-fifteen and still there was light in the west.

David took a deep breath and started for home, praying in the orange light of the sun, half sunken now, still blinding in the rearview, partially blocked by the silhouette of his brother in the passenger seat.

Acknowledgements

The author would like to express his boundless gratitude to the following people for their help with the collection; to Allan Bates, Ben Schneider, Trevor Taylor, Casey Oberto, Frank Mayfield, Peter Meyers, Sam Greene, Grant Papastefan, Charlie Stelnicki, Will Lund, Ryan Deweerdt, Rein Tael, Jacob Bartz, Matt Kastein, Wendy and Joe Taylor, Victor Volkman, Tyler Tichelaar, Joseph D. Haske, and most of all John Austin.

About the Author

J. D. Austin was raised in St. Louis, Missouri and has been moving gradually north since the age of fourteen. After dropping out of college in November of 2019, he worked as a kayak guide, a wedding server, bar security, lighting designer, stage carpenter, ski technician, and in the nursery department at a Home Depot. His fiction has appeared in *The Incandescent Review* and *U.P. Reader Vol. 7*. His first novel, *The Last Huck*, was selected as a UP Notable book for 2024. You can learn more about him at JDAustinStories.com.

Jakob, Niklas and Peter Kinnunen grew up playing together on their family's berry farm on the Keweenaw Peninsula in Michigan's U.P. The three of them inherit the land when their beloved uncle passes away, but Jakob goes to prison and Peter, who goes broke during the 2008 financial crash, calls Niklas and suggests they sell the land for fast cash. Niklas fights back against Peter, but Peter convinces Niklas to take a trip up north, from their homes in Milwaukee, to visit the

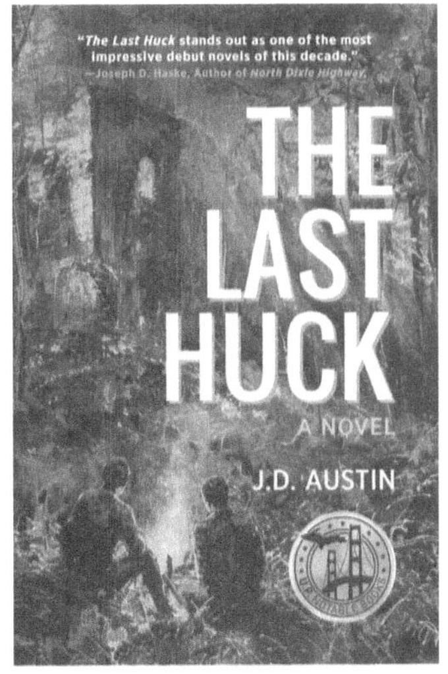

place and get closure. Haunted by their childhoods and the absence of their beloved Jakob, they spend the weekend drinking, fighting, reminiscing and trying to figure out whether or not to sell. Woven together with moments going back four generations, *The Last Huck* is the saga of a family ravaged by time and modernity, yet holding on to one another for dear life.

"In his first novel, J. D. Austin vividly captures the painful conflicts among the young men as they spend one last weekend in places that were the scenes of their happiest childhood memories."
—Jon C. Stott, author, *Summers at the Lake: Upper Michigan Moments and Memories*

"The adventure that ensues not only immediately draws the reader in, but does so in a fashion that makes it virtually impossible to put the book down. It is always a joy for seasoned sojourners to witness young talent, such as J. D. Austin, blossom and flourish as we pass through this life."
—Michael Carrier (MA NYU), author, *Jack Handler* Murder Mysteries / Hardboiled Thrillers